Tumtum & Nutmeg

THE GREAT ESCAPE

by Emily Bearn

Illustrated by Nick Price

EGMONT

Praise for Tumtum & Nutmeg

'Told simply, with charming detail, this old-fashioned and well-published story . . . will delight children who are of an age to relish secret friends and a cosy world in miniature.' *Sunday Times*

'This book is full of fantastic description, whilst not dropping excitement for a minute. Once you start reading it you can't put it down.' Lily, aged 8

'Bearn is a fine writer and her tale . . . is a gently humorous page-turner full of little details . . . Highly recommended.' *Financial Times*

'A stunning debut . . . This is most definitely a candidate for a classic of the future.' LoveReading4Kids

'Bearn's style is as crisp and warm as a home-baked biscuit.' Amanda Craig, *The Times*

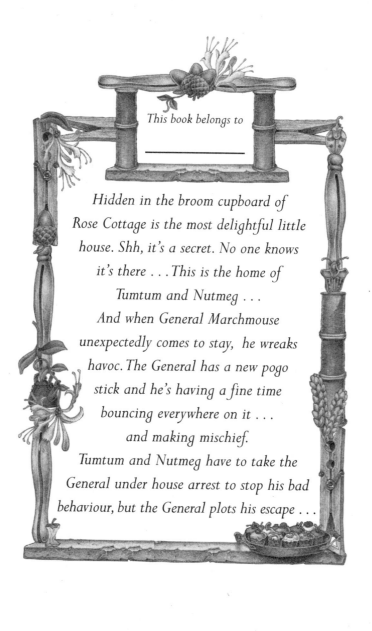

This book belongs to

_____

Hidden in the broom cupboard of
Rose Cottage is the most delightful little
house. Shh, it's a secret. No one knows
it's there . . . This is the home of
Tumtum and Nutmeg . . .
And when General Marchmouse
unexpectedly comes to stay, he wreaks
havoc. The General has a new pogo
stick and he's having a fine time
bouncing everywhere on it . . .
and making mischief.
Tumtum and Nutmeg have to take the
General under house arrest to stop his bad
behaviour, but the General plots his escape . . .

Also by Emily Bearn

Tumtum and Nutmeg

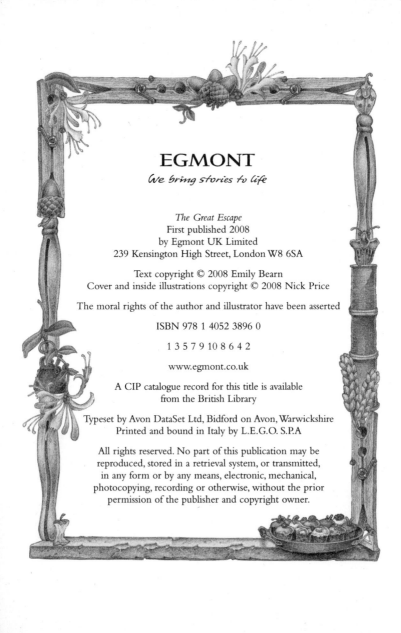

EGMONT

We bring stories to life

The Great Escape
First published 2008
by Egmont UK Limited
239 Kensington High Street, London W8 6SA

Text copyright © 2008 Emily Bearn
Cover and inside illustrations copyright © 2008 Nick Price

The moral rights of the author and illustrator have been asserted

ISBN 978 1 4052 3896 0

1 3 5 7 9 10 8 6 4 2

www.egmont.co.uk

A CIP catalogue record for this title is available
from the British Library

Typeset by Avon DataSet Ltd, Bidford on Avon, Warwickshire
Printed and bound in Italy by L.E.G.O. S.P.A

For my father

Chapter One

For Mr and Mrs Nutmouse, of Nutmouse Hall, the day had begun much like any other. Mrs Nutmouse (who was known as Nutmeg, on account of her having nutmeg hair) had leapt out of bed at dawn, and raced downstairs to bustle and bake and clean. And Mr Nutmouse (who was known as Tumtum, on account of his having such a large one) had stayed tucked up under the covers until he heard the bell ring for breakfast.

He tumbled down to the kitchen in his dressing gown. 'Good morning, dear!' he said dozily, as Nutmeg helped him to porridge and toast and scrambled eggs and bacon, and a pancake or two. 'Now, let's see. What shall we do today?'

Tumtum always asked this, even though he knew quite well what the answer would be. For although they lived in a big, grand house, the Nutmouses led very simple lives.

For the most part, Nutmeg spent her days scuttling and bustling in the kitchen, preparing delicious things to eat. And Tumtum spent his days in the library, warming his toes in front of the fire.

So Tumtum knew what Nutmeg's answer would be. 'I think I'll scuttle and bustle in the

kitchen, dear,' she said.

'Good idea!' he replied. 'And I'll toast my toes in the library.'

Nutmeg approved of this plan, so they both settled down to eat, looking forward to another peaceful day at Nutmouse Hall.

But just as Nutmeg was refilling the teapot, there was a loud 'Rap! Tap! Tap!' on the front door.

'I wonder who that could be?' Tumtum asked warily. Nutmeg followed him through to the hall, feeling just as puzzled. The post mouse was the only person who tended to visit at this hour, but today was a Sunday.

Before Tumtum had time to draw the bolts, the 'Rap! Tap! Tapping!' started again. Then they

heard a loud voice on the other side of the door.

'It's General Marchmouse!' announced General Marchmouse, speaking in a very General Marchmousely way.

'*The General!*' Nutmeg whispered, looking at Tumtum in astonishment. 'What on earth can he want?'

'I can't imagine, dear,' Tumtum replied. For it was most unlike the General to visit so early.

'What a nice surprise, General!' he said when he opened the door.

And in some ways it was, for the Nutmouses were very fond of the General. (Who was known to everyone as General, on account of him being rather Generalish.) But in other ways it wasn't, for while Tumtum and Nutmeg were very quiet mice, the General was an unusually noisy one.

And today he was at his noisiest. He marched into the hall and thumped two leather suitcases on the floor. 'Hello!' he said heartily. 'Would you be so kind as to let me stay a night or two?'

'Why, er – of course, General!' Tumtum stammered, feeling he couldn't very well refuse.

'Good,' the General replied. 'Mrs Marchmouse has gone to stay with her old nanny for a week and I was feeling lonely racketing about the gun cupboard on my own. Now that I'm retired from active service, time can hang a little heavy, you know. So I thought to myself, *How jolly it would be to spend a few days with my dear friends the Nutmouses, at Nutmouse Hall!*'

Tumtum and Nutmeg both groaned inwardly.

There was no hope of a quiet day now.

'What's that?' Nutmeg asked, noticing that the General was carrying a fat silver pole.

'That is a pogo stick,' the General replied proudly. 'The Royal Mouse Army's new secret weapon.'

'Whatever do you mean?' Tumtum asked.

The General looked at him down his nose, thinking him very ill-informed.

'Haven't you read *The Mouse Times*, Nutmouse?' he asked. 'The army is being modernised. The soldiers are no longer going to ride squirrels – oh, squirrels are old hat! From now on, the cavalry will bounce into battle on sleek, silver pogo sticks, just like this. Stand back, Nutty, and I'll show you how it's done.'

Then the General mounted his stick, and started to bounce – boung! boung! boung! – round the hall. Then he bounced – boung! boung! boung! – round the drawing room, and the billiard room, and the ballroom. And so he went on, bouncing all round Nutmouse Hall, knocking into lamps and tables and stuffed cockroaches, and generally making a thorough nuisance of himself.

By the time he reached the kitchen, he was bouncing so high that he biffed his head on the ceiling. He sat down to breakfast feeling quite dizzy.

'We mustn't let him out of our sight for a minute,' Tumtum whispered to his wife. 'We don't want him giving us away.'

Nutmeg nodded anxiously. Any mouse

visiting Nutmouse Hall had to come and go very carefully, for it was a secret house, which no human knew about. It had been built long ago in the broom cupboard of a scruffy cottage called Rose Cottage, which was lived in by two scruffy children called Arthur and Lucy Mildew, and their even scruffier father.

None of the Mildews knew they had a broom cupboard behind their kitchen wall, because there had always been a big wooden dresser hiding the cupboard door. The Nutmouses' front gates were behind the dresser, and they were forever creeping in and out across the Mildews' kitchen floor.

But the Mildews had never seen them, because Tumtum and Nutmeg crept very quietly.

And they did most of their creeping at night.

At night they crept all over the place. They crept into the larder, and into Mr Mildew's study, and sometimes they crept up to the attic, where Arthur and Lucy slept, and did all sorts of helpful things. Nutmeg darned the children's clothes, and tidied their satchels, and polished their shoes with a mop; and once Tumtum had mended the wings on Arthur's model plane.

Now and again, the children and Nutmeg wrote letters to each other, which they left on the chest of drawers. But the children had no idea that Nutmeg was a mouse. In one of her letters she had told them that she was a fairy – so that's what they thought she was. The Nutmouses knew that Arthur and Lucy must never learn the truth. For some humans have funny feelings about mice, and think they shouldn't be allowed in the house.

And imagine what the children would think if they saw the General bouncing about on a pogo stick.

'We must keep him constantly entertained,' Tumtum whispered to Nutmeg. 'Then he might just forget about this pogoing nonsense.'

'What would you like to do this morning, General?' he asked jovially, turning to his friend. 'We could have a game of chess!'

'Later, perhaps,' the General replied, dabbing scrambled egg from his whiskers. 'First I shall go exploring. The broom cupboard's not big enough for a mouse on a pogo stick. I want to have a bounce around the Mildews' kitchen floor, and see if they've left any good pickings.'

This was not what Tumtum wanted to hear.

'Now, look here, General. I don't think that's wise,' he said. 'You'll only draw attention to yourself. And besides, the Mildews never leave good pickings. They eat horrible things like tinned spaghetti. That's why we have our food delivered by the grocery mouse.'

'Well I'd like to try tinned spaghetti,' the General said carelessly. 'Anyway, I won't be gone long. Just a quick breath of fresh air, and I'll be home in time for tea.'

Tumtum looked stern. (He did not often look stern, but when he did he looked very stern indeed.)

'General, so long as you are our guest, Rose

Cottage is out of bounds,' he said firmly. 'Now please promise me that you will not set foot outside the broom cupboard. We've thirty-six rooms here in Nutmouse Hall — surely that's enough for any mouse to bounce about in.'

'Oh, all right then,' the General muttered — for Tumtum did look rather fierce. 'I promise. I shall pogo around here instead.'

As far as Tumtum was concerned, the matter was closed. For a promise is a promise, after all.

But General Marchmouse found this particular promise very hard to keep.

The General was a mouse who craved adventures, but since retiring from the army he'd found them in increasingly short supply. He was starved of danger — and he had a feeling that by pogoing around Rose Cottage he might finally find some.

And yet he was a mouse of honour, so of course he could never go back on his word. That would be out of the question.

Huff! How tiresome to have to stay indoors! he thought crossly, helping himself to the last rasher of bacon. He was still full of energy, so when breakfast was over he mounted his pogo stick again, and started crashing about in the ballroom.

'Bullseye!' he cried, as he went smack-bang into a marble statue. He made as much noise as possible hoping that Tumtum would get so fed up he'd let him go. But though Tumtum could hear the racket from the library, he said nothing, which made the General even more frustrated.

'Come on Nutmouse. Surely it wouldn't do any harm if I went out for a few minutes?' he began, as they sat down to a light lunch of earwig pie. But Tumtum would not back down.

'I have already made my feelings clear, and I have no more to say on the matter.'

The General glared at him – then he finally let the subject drop.

But after lunch, when Tumtum had disappeared to the library, and while Nutmeg was bustling in the kitchen, the General found himself wandering into the hall, with his pogo stick tucked under his arm. He stood there awhile, looking longingly at the front door. 'You gave your word,' the Generalish side of him said. But the adventurous side said, '*Go on!*'

And so on he went.

He crept out of the door, then tiptoed towards the Nutmouses' front gates. He let himself out and fumbled his way through the cobwebs underneath the dresser. Then he marched out into the kitchen, feeling a delicious thrill of adventure now that he was out of bounds.

It was a foolhardy time to set out, for it was broad daylight, and someone might easily have spotted him. But the General could hear Arthur and Lucy outside, playing in the garden. So he assumed he would be safe.

'I'm king of the roost!' he cried, bouncing gleefully across the kitchen floor.

He had visited Rose Cottage several times

before, and he knew exactly where he wanted to go. He bounced into the hall, then, gritting his teeth, he bounced up the stairs and on to the landing. Then he stopped suddenly, hearing something clattering in the study.

He hopped across the carpet and poked his nose under the door.

Inside, Mr Mildew – who was an inventor, but not a very successful one – was sitting on the floor, amid a sea of tiny wires and twisted bits of metal. He was trying to invent a mechanical frog that could be programmed to catch flies in its mouth. But like most of Mr Mildew's inventions, it was all going wrong. And as a result he was pounding his fists on the floor in a hopeless rage.

The General watched for a moment, then he

turned around and bounced across the landing, until he was standing beneath the steep flight of steps leading to the attic. He flung his pogo stick on to the bottom step and heaved himself up after it.

I'll have all the toys to myself, he thought excitedly, as he huffed and puffed his way upstairs. *I'll make castles out of building bricks, and tie up the teddy bears! Oh, lucky old me!*

But even the fearless General Marchmouse might have hesitated a moment had he realised just what sort of adventures were in store.

Chapter Two

The General finally hoisted himself over the top step, on to the attic floor. He was drenched in sweat, and the belt of his camouflage trousers was cutting into him. 'You must go on a diet, Marchmouse,' he muttered, searching in his pocket for a humbug. He got to his feet, crunching it noisily. But then he saw something that made him suck in his breath.

He was looking straight into the barrel of a rifle.

The General was so frightened he could feel his knees wobble. Standing before him was a figure in red uniform, with a visor hiding his face. It wasn't the uniform of the Royal Mouse Army – and though the soldier was the size of a mouse, he didn't have a tail.

'Do you know who I am?' the General demanded, trying to disguise his terror. 'Well, I'll tell you. I am General Marchmouse . . . So . . . er, well . . . So there you have it!'

The soldier ignored him, which made the General cross. Generals are not used to being ignored.

'With whose army do you serve?' the

General asked briskly, but there was no reply. And that made the General even crosser.

'Where is your commanding officer? I shall report you for insubordination!' he shouted. He was so cross he forgot he was frightened.

But still there was no reply.

'I HAVE KILLED A RAT WITH MY OWN BARE PAWS!' the General roared, determined to impress him.

But the soldier did not respond.

So General Marchmouse did something very un-Generalish. He reached forward, and punched him in the stomach.

But, to his astonishment, the soldier just toppled over.

The General blushed, feeling very foolish.

For suddenly he realised that it was a toy soldier, made of tin! And now, looking around him, he could see dozens more of them, scattered all about the floor. Some were in red uniforms, and some in khaki. There were tanks too, and piles of sandbags and grenades, and there were machine guns the size of matches.

The General sucked in his breath, hardly able to believe his luck. A whole battlefield stretched before him – and everything was mouse-sized! At last, he could come out of retirement, and take command! Oh, how he throbbed with delight!

I'll form the men into lines, and command a full-scale offensive, he thought gleefully. *We'll blow up the doll's house!*

So the General spent a blissful hour ordering

his new regiments. The doll's house was placed under siege, and its front door barricaded with a pencil box. The red soldiers were put inside to defend it, firing from the windows and the roof, while the khaki soldiers advanced on the building in platoons. The General commanded operations standing on top of one of Lucy's ballet shoes, shouting, 'Fire!' until he was nearly hoarse.

When he had hurled all the plastic grenades, he went to rummage in the toy box, looking for more missiles. He nibbled through the string of one of Lucy's necklaces, and scooped the beads into his kit bag. Then he returned to his post on the ballet shoe and started lobbing them at the doll's house, one by one. He was not a good shot, so he didn't succeed in breaking any windows.

But the beads made a satisfying clonk as they smashed against the wall.

When he'd tired of that, he decided to have a go on Arthur's train set. The tracks, which had been painstakingly repaired by Tumtum, looped all round the floor, and every half metre or so they sloped up and down in steep ramps.

I could get up quite a speed! he thought excitedly. He jumped on his pogo stick and hopped over a bank of sandbags towards the glistening blue carriages.

'Sorry, old boy,' he grunted, yanking a toy soldier from the driver's compartment. 'But General Marchmouse is taking command.'

He sat on the stool, and turned the big red switch to 'On'. There was a gentle rumbling noise, then the train slowly heaved into motion.

The General whooped with delight and started grabbing wildly at the controls, trying to make it go faster. 'Faster! Faster!' he roared – but Arthur's train ran on a small battery, and however much the General punched and shoved at the knobs, it kept to the same steady speed.

Let's see what happens if I freewheel, he thought impatiently.

The train chugged round a bedpost, then climbed to the top of the biggest hump in the tracks, which was nearly as high as the doll's house. The General hunched himself over the gear stick, then gingerly reached out a paw, and switched off the engine. The train wobbled a moment, then it lurched forward, and started whooshing downhill.

The General clung to the wheel, shrieking with glee as the room sped past his window in a dizzying blur.

'Clear the tracks!' he shouted, blasting the horn. 'General Marchmouse is bringing reinforcements!'

But then he saw the hairpin bend in the track just in front of him.

He grappled in panic for the brake, but the train just hurtled on faster. 'Help! *Help!*' he squealed, cowering into a ball on the carriage floor, his paws pressed to his ears. He felt the train lurch violently as it hit the curve, and then the driver's compartment skidded off the rails, and sailed into the air. The General fell nose down against the window, and saw his tin regiments spread out below him on the floor. 'I'm flying!' he trembled.

But the worst was still to come. For the next moment everything went black, as the carriage smashed on to the roof of the doll's house.

The General lay there, too dazed to move. At first he could see nothing but stars and flashing lights. Then, little by little, the room came back into focus. But everything was upside down.

Gradually, as he came to his senses, he realised what had happened. The carriage had landed on its side, and he was squashed tight beneath the driver's stool, with all four paws in the air. The door was on top of him, where the ceiling should be. So it was no wonder everything looked topsy turvy.

'Oh, poor old me,' he whimpered. 'What a

pretty pickle!'

But, as he was lying there, feeling as sorry for himself as any mouse can feel, he heard something which made everything much worse. Arthur and Lucy were coming up the stairs.

Chapter Three

The General listened in terror as the children's voices got closer and closer. He knew he was in dreadful danger. Arthur would be astonished enough to discover that his train had been derailed. But what would he do when he found a mouse at the wheel? The General did not know Arthur as well as the Nutmouses did, and he imagined there might be terrible punishments in store.

Gritting his teeth, for he was very sore, he grasped his pogo stick and used it to smash open the door above his head. Then he wriggled free of the steering wheel and pulled himself upright. Peeking outside, he saw that the carriage was stranded high on the doll's house roof, lodged between two chimneys.

He gripped the door frame and hauled himself out on to the rooftop, wincing with pain. He tried to run, using his pogo stick as a crutch, but the roof was steep and he kept slipping. He floundered about desperately, but there was nowhere to hide. 'I'll never surrender!' he vowed — and as Arthur and Lucy entered the room he tossed his pogo stick down a chimney and dived after it headfirst.

*

The children got a terrible fright when they saw the soldiers pointing their guns out of the doll's house windows, and the train lying on the roof.

Lucy assumed it must have been Arthur's doing, and Arthur assumed it must have been Lucy's doing, and there were some cross words exchanged. But Arthur pointed out that it couldn't have been him, because he'd been outside all afternoon. And Lucy pointed out that it couldn't have been her because she'd been outside all afternoon too.

So who was it? Surely not Nutmeg, for fairies didn't do things like this. And it couldn't have been their father, for fathers don't crash their children's trains.

'There must be another fairy, as well as Nutmeg,' Arthur said. 'A bad fairy, who makes a

mess. An elf – of sorts.'

The children considered this a while. Neither of them would have believed in any sort of fairy a year ago, but since acquiring Nutmeg they had become more open-minded.

'I wonder if Nutmeg knows,' Lucy said. 'Do you think we should tell her?'

'I suppose so,' Arthur said. 'Let's leave everything as it is so she can see for herself what whoever it is has done. Imagine how surprised she'll be when she finds soldiers firing out of her doll's house.'

They both considered it to be Nutmeg's doll's house because she had redecorated it from top to bottom with new curtains and carpets and cushion covers. She had even made a tapestry cover for the piano stool. And though they had never seen her, they suspected she sometimes spent the night there, for she kept a pair of slippers in its bedroom.

So Lucy found some paper, and the children sat together on the floor and composed a letter:

Dear Nutmeg,

We think an elf has been in the attic while we were outside. He crashed Arthur's train, and broke Lucy's necklace, and he attacked the doll's house with tin soldiers. And he's eaten all the tea we left out for you. What do you think we should do?

Love from,

Arthur and Lucy.

When they had finished, Lucy folded the letter in

half and left it propped against a hairbrush on the chest of drawers.

'I hope she does something to stop it,' Lucy said.

'So do I,' Arthur agreed. He was beginning to feel quite hostile to whoever had crashed his train.

While all this was going on, the General was in considerable discomfort. By a stroke of misfortune he had dived down the drawing room chimney, which was the longest of all the chimneys in the doll's house. His pogo stick had clattered down to the hearth, but he was too fat to follow, and he had got stuck halfway down. He wriggled and squirmed, but he couldn't budge – he was wedged upside down, with his stomach squashed tight against the chimney bricks.

In this undignified position, he had listened to the children's conversation, feeling crosser and crosser.

'An *elf*!' he fumed, kicking his legs. 'I'll teach you to refer to the great General Marchmouse as *an elf*!' But though he protested loudly, the children couldn't hear a thing, because mice have such small voices that even when they are shouting they only make a tiny squeal. And besides, the General's shouts were muffled by the chimney.

By the time the children went downstairs for tea, the General could shout no more. He pulled in his stomach, trying to calculate how tightly he was stuck. *I'll have to lose at least half an ounce before*

I can squeeze out of here, he thought miserably. *And that would mean starving for three days.*

It was a very glum thought.

Chapter Four

It had been a peaceful afternoon in Nutmouse Hall. After lunch, Nutmeg had scuttled to the sewing room to start work on a velvet smock for one of Lucy's dolls, and Tumtum had pottered off to the library to put his feet up.

I shall have a nice long read, he had thought, flopping in an armchair in front of the fire. But the fire was so warm, and Tumtum's tumtum was so full of lunch, that it wasn't long before he had fallen fast asleep.

All through the house, there was not a sound to be heard save for the 'tick tock' of the big clock in the hall. Nutmeg was so absorbed in her work that she hardly noticed the afternoon slipping by.

'Goodness,' she said eventually, looking at her watch. 'It's gone teatime, and I haven't even iced the fairy cakes.' So she hurried downstairs. But when she reached the hall, she noticed that the front door had been left open.

That's odd, she thought, for she knew that Tumtum was very particular about closing it. And all of a sudden a horrible thought occurred to her.

'Oh, surely not,' she whispered. '*Surely* the

General wouldn't have broken his promise!' But something made her go outside and check the front gates.

And they were open too.

She raced back indoors, calling the General's name and, getting no reply, she ran upstairs to look for him in his room.

But neither the General nor his pogo stick were there.

'Tumtum! Wake up! Oh, wake up! The General's gone!' Nutmeg cried, bursting into the library.

'Gone, dear?' Tumtum muttered sleepily, rubbing his eyes.

'Yes, gone, dear!' Nutmeg cried. 'Gone bouncing round Rose Cottage, dear!'

'But he can't have gone,' Tumtum said. 'He promised he wouldn't leave the broom cupboard.'

'Oh, promises, promises!' Nutmeg wailed. 'He's gone, Tumtum. We must get him back before he's seen!'

Tumtum prised himself to his feet and followed his wife to the front gates. Just as Nutmeg had said, they had been left wide open, swinging in the draught. And from the other side of the wall the Nutmouses could hear Mr Mildew talking on the telephone.

'Well, we can't set out to look for him now,' Tumtum said firmly. 'Three mice would be much more conspicuous than one. The General will come home as soon as he gets hungry, we can be sure of that. We must just pray that no one sees him bouncing back under the dresser.'

Nutmeg agreed, but there followed an agonising wait. They sat in the kitchen, listening hopefully for the sound of the General 'Rap! Tap! Tapping!' at the front door. But supper time came and went – and still there was no sign of him.

'It's most unlike him to miss a meal,' Nutmeg said eventually. 'He must be in some sort of trouble.'

'I suppose we'll have to go and look for him – he's been gone for ages,' Tumtum said. 'But we'd better wait another hour, then everyone will have gone to bed.'

'He may be injured,' Nutmeg said. 'I'll bring some bandages in case he needs patching up.'

So at ten o'clock, after an anxious cup of

cocoa, the Nutmouses finally set out to track the General down.

Tumtum held Nutmeg's paw as they groped their way under the dresser, for he knew it made her shiver to feel the cobwebs brushing against her legs. Nutmeg was a little wary of the Rose Cottage spiders, for some of them were bigger than she was.

The Mildews' kitchen was very dark. The curtains were closed, and the downstairs lights had been turned off.

Tumtum shone his torch round the room, to be sure that there was no one lurking. Then they scurried through every nook and cranny, calling the General's name. They looked for him in the cupboards and the cutlery drawers, and in the saucepans and the teacups; then they hunted in the laundry basket and the vegetable rack. They even explored inside Arthur's wellington boots.

When they had searched the kitchen they searched the hall, then the sitting room, then the upstairs landing, and then the bathroom. And drawing a blank there, they crept into the study, and searched that too – while Mr Mildew lay snoring on the sofa, clutching one of the legs of his mechanical frog.

'We'd better check the children's room,' Tumtum said finally. 'There's nowhere else he could be.'

So, with much huffing and puffing, for they were getting very tired, the Nutmouses started clambering up the attic stairs.

Arthur and Lucy were sound asleep, for it was long past their bedtime. But the Nutmouses entered the room on tiptoe just in case. When Tumtum was sure the children were sleeping, he turned on his torch and shone it over the floor. And they were both astonished at what they saw.

'Oh!' Nutmeg cried, gazing round her in dismay. She had tidied the room only last night, but now it looked like a battlefield. 'Whatever could have happened?' she asked.

Tumtum put his arm around her, feeling equally bewildered. It didn't occur to them that the General could be responsible for such a mess.

They stood in silence, surveying the chaos. Then suddenly they heard a noise which made them jump. It was the sort of noise a ghost might make – a long, muffled 'Aaaaah'. They both stiffened, and pricked their ears. There was a brief silence, then they heard it again – but it was louder this time.

'It's coming from the doll's house,' said Nutmeg. 'Look! The door's been left open!'

They crept towards it, glancing warily at the tin soldiers firing from the windows. Then they poked their heads into the hall. The moaning had started up again and it sounded much closer now.

'It's coming from in there,' Tumtum said, gesturing towards the drawing room. They tiptoed together through the door. 'Gracious,' Tumtum said, pointing to the hearth. 'It's the General's pogo stick!'

No sooner had he spoken than they heard another groan – but this time, instead of 'Aaaaah', it sounded like, '*Heeeelp Meeeee!*' And it was echoing down the chimney.

Tumtum crouched in the fireplace and shone his torch up, to discover a very wretched-looking General Marchmouse, suspended upside down.

'General!' Tumtum cried. 'Whatever are you doing?'

'I am hanging upside down!' the General said furiously. 'Can't you see? I've been stuck here all afternoon. Now pull me down, won't you? *Pull me down!*'

The General stretched out a paw, and Tumtum grasped it as tight as he could, and pulled and pulled. Then Nutmeg held on to Tumtum, and she pulled too. And finally, with Tumtum and Nutmeg both pulling with all their might, the

General thudded into the grate.

'Ooooh!' he moaned feebly. 'I thought I'd starve to death!'

'How on earth did you get up there, General?' Tumtum asked, heaving him to his feet.

'I was hiding,' the General said miserably, rubbing the bruise on the end of his nose. 'I'd had a perfectly pleasant afternoon commanding the tin soldiers in battle, then I decided to take Arthur's train for a spin, but the tiresome thing crashed, and just as I was crawling out of the wreckage –'

'So it was *YOU* who caused all this mayhem, General!' Tumtum said furiously. 'When we saw the mess, we thought rats had broken in. But it was *YOU*! What a fine way to carry on! You break your word of honour, and then you come up here and

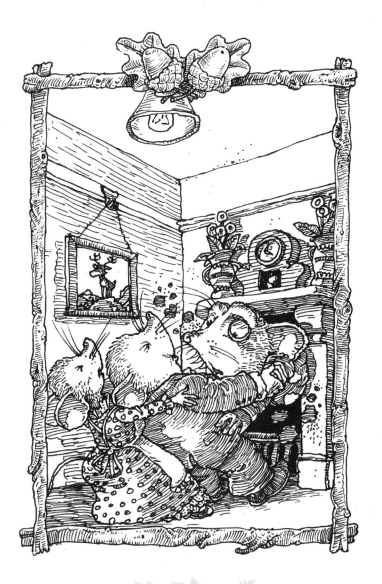

wreak havoc with Arthur and Lucy's toys! It is hardly the sort of behaviour one expects from an officer and a gentlemouse!'

The General, who had been expecting sympathy, flushed angrily. But before he could utter a word of protest Tumtum had thrust an arm under his shoulders, and was marching him across the floor.

'I'm sorry, General,' he said grimly. 'But you're coming back to Nutmouse Hall – under house arrest!'

Chapter Five

As Tumtum was leading his indignant prisoner towards the steps, Nutmeg noticed the letter addressed to her on the children's chest of drawers. She quickly scrambled up to it, climbing by means of the various socks and tights and jersey sleeves tumbling from the drawers.

She was terrified the children might have caught sight of the General before he flung himself down the doll's house chimney. So she was anxious to see what the letter would say.

But when she read it, her mind was put at rest.

'An elf!' she chuckled, reading in the glow of Lucy's alarm clock. 'So they think General Marchmouse is an elf. Goodness, what would all the mice in the village think?'

She at once dashed back into the doll's house and sat down at the desk in the drawing room where she kept her stationery. She had her main desk at Nutmouse Hall, but this was the one she used when she wrote to the children. There was even a little light on it, which she needed on nights such as this, when there was no moon to see by.

She took a piece of paper from the drawer then dipped her pen in the ink pot and composed the following reply:

Dear Arthur and Lucy,

I am sorry for all the mess the naughty elf has caused, but I will come and tidy it up tomorrow night. I believe I know the elf concerned, and I promise he won't come back. You need not do a thing.

Love,

Nutmeg.

She put the letter in an envelope, and addressed it to 'Arthur and Lucy Mildew, The Attic, Rose Cottage'. (Her writing was so small that the children always had to read her letters with a

magnifying glass.) She stuffed it in the pocket of her apron, then climbed back up the chest of drawers and propped it against Lucy's hairbrush. After that, she rushed off to catch up with Tumtum, who had already dragged his prisoner back to Nutmouse Hall.

The Nutmouses determined to keep Nutmeg's promise, and to prevent the General from ever returning to the attic. So Tumtum padlocked the front gates, and he kept the key to the padlock on a string round his neck so as to be sure the General could not get his paws on it.

They had expected him to be furious at being held prisoner, but he appeared to take it quite well.

On Monday, which was the first day of his captivity, he seemed restless, and pogoed round and round the ballroom. But on Tuesday he was much calmer, and by Wednesday he gave the impression he was enjoying his quiet life. He helped Nutmeg make a kedgeree in the morning, then he ate a magnificent lunch, and spent the afternoon dozing in the library.

'I do so like these peaceful spring days,' Tumtum said, as he led his guest into dinner that evening.

'Quite so,' the General agreed. 'A peaceful day is just the sort of day I like.'

Tumtum was very pleased to hear this. But in actual fact the General hated peaceful days, and he was not feeling nearly as settled as he would have

Tumtum believe.

He was secretly still fuming at being held hostage, and was longing to get back to the attic. He may have been battered and bruised by his adventures, but every bone in his body ached for another ride on Arthur's train set, and another chance to lob toy grenades at the doll's house.

So his relaxed manner was just a ploy while he plotted his escape. He had been thinking of all sorts of bold and foolish schemes. He could smash through the Nutmouses' gates with a battering ram! Or blast them open with gun-powder!

But since he didn't have a battering ram, nor any gun-powder, he was unlikely to succeed.

Then finally, shortly before dinner, he had come up with what he considered to be a much more sensible plan . . .

'How about a game of scrabble?' Tumtum asked when they had finished pudding.

The General yawned theatrically. 'Truth be told, I'm feeling a bit sluggish,' he said. 'I think I'll go to bed and read a learned book.'

'Good idea!' Tumtum said approvingly, thinking he might do just the same. 'Sleep tight, then.'

'Sleep tight,' the General replied. Then he walked upstairs, humming a little tune. But instead of going to his room, he loitered on the landing. And as soon as he heard the Nutmouses going into the library with their tray of cocoa, he slid gleefully down the banister, and slipped out of the front door.

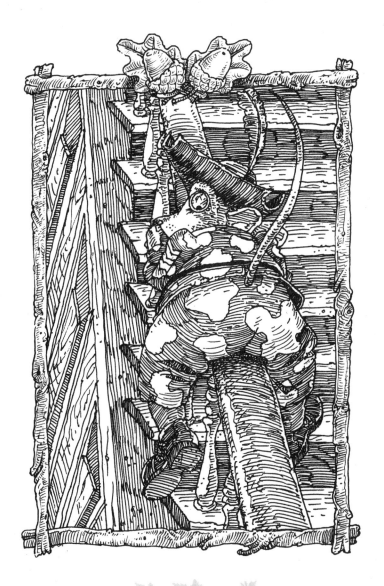

He had hidden his pogo stick among the croquet mallets. He picked it up and started hopping purposefully across the broom cupboard floor.

But he did not head for the gates, for he knew they were locked. Instead, he bounced round Nutmouse Hall towards the broom cupboard's back wall. High up in that wall was a little window, and it was through that window that the General intended to escape.

It was far above his head, and the wall much too smooth for him to climb. But the General had an ambitious plan.

Pressing down on the foot rest as hard as he could, he pogoed back and forth on the floor, each bounce carrying him higher and higher, until he was bouncing so high he could see a fly cruising in the air below him.

He bounced back off the floor and soared higher still – and when he was level with the window he let go of his pogo stick and grabbed the sill with both paws. He clung to it for dear life, and heard the stick clatter to the floor beneath him.

There could be no going back now.

With gritted teeth, he hoisted up his elbows and heaved himself on to the ledge. *No one can make a prisoner of me!* he thought, as he stood looking down triumphantly on the rooftops of Nutmouse Hall.

He wriggled out through the little crack in the windowpane, then clambered down the honeysuckle to the ground. 'General Marchmouse

strikes again,' he chuckled as he marched along beside the wall. Then he held in his stomach and crawled into Rose Cottage under the garden door.

Chapter Six

Mr Mildew was sitting at the kitchen table, but the General crept across the floor behind him and reached the hall unseen. The children were still up – he could hear their voices carrying from the sitting room. It was just as he had hoped – he would have all the toys to himself.

But when he arrived in the attic, he found that everything was amiss. The soldiers he had lined up in battle had all been swept to one side. And his sandbags had been dumped in the toy box.

What cheek! he thought, furious that the children should have interfered with his battle scene. He rolled up his sleeves and began to drag his troops back into position. He arranged the khaki soldiers in crescents around the floor, then he hauled the red ones into the doll's house.

He was dripping with sweat, and his camouflages felt unbearably hot. There was only one thing for it. He would have to strip off.

No one will see me, he thought, hastily removing his jacket and trousers. When he had undressed down to his underpants, he felt much more comfortable.

'Back to work!' he grunted, and started

lugging a soldier up the doll's house stairs. He stood him on the landing, shooting down towards the front door. Then he heaved another into the bedroom. 'Pow!' he shouted, pointing its rifle out of the window –

But then he reeled back in fright. For peering in at him was a huge, human eye.

It was Lucy, and she got a fright too, as any child might who discovered a mouse playing in her doll's house.

'Oh!' she cried.

But though she was very taken aback, she was still quicker witted than the General. While he stood rooted to the spot, she shot out a hand and shut the bedroom window, then snapped the latch down on the outside.

'Arthur, look what's in here — a mouse wearing underpants!'

The General panicked, and stumbled out of the bedroom towards the stairs; but by the time he got to the ground floor Lucy had secured the other windows too, and bolted the doll's house door.

He was trapped.

Arthur came and crouched next to his sister, and they both peered inside, watching in astonishment as the little brown mouse stamped his feet in rage, demanding to be let out.

'He's the one who's been playing with my soldiers!' Arthur said, seeing the tin man on the doll's house landing, and the sandbags piled by the door. First a fairy, and now a mouse in underpants! There seemed to be no end of

extraordinary things going on in the attic.

The General was rattling the windows now, and kicking furiously at the front door. 'We mustn't let him go,' said Lucy. 'He might cause even more damage.'

'But we can't just leave him in the doll's house,' said Arthur. 'He'll keep us awake all night scrabbling.'

The children sat in silence a moment, wondering what to do.

'I've got an idea!' Lucy said finally. 'Just for today, let's put him in a biscuit tin. We can pierce holes in it, so he can breathe, and give him some food and water. And we can leave the tin in the kitchen overnight, so he doesn't keep us awake. Then tomorrow morning we'll take him to school, and put him in Pets' House. He'll have a lovely time there.'

Arthur at once agreed, for Pets' House was a very agreeable place. It was a big wire cage, and all sorts of animals had lived in it. Once there had been a guinea pig called Sam, but eventually he'd died of old age, and then two hamsters had moved in. But one holiday the hamsters had gone to live with the headmistress, Miss Page, and she had got on with them so well that she'd decided to keep them at home. And after that two gerbils had arrived, but they'd had lots of children, and some of their children had had children too, so at the present time there were twelve of them living in the cage.

'Good idea. He's bound to like living with

gerbils – they're just the same size as him,' Arthur said confidently. 'I'll go and look for a tin.'

Hearing this, the General became even more frantic. 'Gerbils!' he cried in horror, hurling himself desperately against the front door. 'They're sending me to live with *gerbils*! Oh, the shame of it!'

Lucy stood guard at the doll's house, making soothing noises, while Arthur raced downstairs. A few minutes later, he returned carrying a purple tin with 'Scottish Oatcakes' written on the side. He poked three holes in the lid with a compass, and Lucy made a bed inside out of old socks.

Then the children took two bowls from the doll's house, and filled one with breadcrumbs and the other with water.

'He'll be very comfortable in there,' Lucy said. Then she opened the drawing room window, and reached a hand inside.

The General cowered behind the sofa with his paws over his eyes. 'Not a biscuit tin!' he begged. 'Oh please don't put me in a dark, dank biscuit tin!' But his protests went unheard. He felt a sudden brush on his spine, and next thing he knew he was being raised into the air, clasped in Lucy's fist. Then everything went dark as he was dumped in his tin prison, and the lid shut on him.

'Let me out! I demand to be let out!' he cried furiously, as the children carried him downstairs to the kitchen. 'Do you know who I am?'

But of course the children didn't know;

and though the great General Marchmouse shouted with all his might, they heard only a tiny squeak.

Much later, when he'd squealed and ranted all he could, the General collapsed on his bed of socks, and sank his head in his paws. He thought longingly of his wife, Mrs Marchmouse, and of their comfortable little home in the gun cupboard, and he wondered if he would ever see his own bed again.

And when he remembered what was in store for him the next day, he felt quite cold. '*Gerbils!*' he kept muttering in horror. '*Gerbils!* I'm going to be sent to live with *gerbils!*' The General had never met a gerbil before, but he'd been told that they were savage creatures, who went around naked, and ate with their paws.

He didn't like the sound of them at all.

Chapter Seven

The General spent a wretched night, tossing and turning in his tin prison. He kept shouting for Tumtum and Nutmeg, praying they would come out looking for him again, as they had before. But his cries were in vain, for the Nutmouses were sound asleep in Nutmouse Hall, with no inkling of what was going on.

And when Nutmeg went downstairs next

morning to cook breakfast, she still didn't suspect a thing. The General had seemed so weary after dinner last night, she supposed he was having a lie-in.

That will be just what he needs, she thought approvingly, melting a knob of butter in her frying pan. *No doubt he'll wake up when he smells the kippers cooking.*

But at eight o'clock, when Nutmeg rang the bell for breakfast, the General did not appear.

'I'd let him sleep on, if I were you,' Tumtum said, helping himself to kedgeree. 'He must have worn himself out with that silly carry-on in the attic.'

'But if he doesn't come down soon his breakfast will spoil,' Nutmeg fussed. 'I've an idea. I shall take him a cup of tea in bed. That should wake him up.'

So she laid a tray with a pot of tea and a jug of milk and a bowl of sugar, and made her way upstairs.

But when she knocked on the General's door, there was no reply.

I hope he's not unwell, she thought.

She knocked again – and when he still didn't answer she opened the door a crack and peeked inside.

And what she saw gave her such a start that she dropped her tray. 'Tumtum!' she shrieked, bursting back into the kitchen. '*The General's gone*!'

'Whatever do you mean, dear?' he said. 'He can't have gone, I locked the front gate.'

'Well he's not in his room, and he clearly

didn't sleep there last night,' Nutmeg cried. 'The bedcovers aren't even rumpled.'

'Well he won't have got far,' Tumtum said. 'He can't have opened the front gate without the key. And there's no other way out. So he must be here somewhere.'

Tumtum abandoned his breakfast, and they started racing round Nutmouse Hall, looking for the General. But though they searched in each of their thirty-six rooms, he was nowhere to be found.

Then they went out of the front door, and saw his pogo stick lying on the broom cupboard floor, under the window. And the same incredible thought occurred to them both.

'He couldn't have bounced that high, surely

. . . it would be . . . it would be quite impossible,' Tumtum stammered.

'Nothing is impossible for General Marchmouse,' Nutmeg said despairingly. 'He must have made a great bounce for freedom after dinner, when he told us he was going upstairs to read in bed. I'll bet he's spent the night in the doll's house, and now he's most likely running amok with Arthur's soldiers. Oh, I do hope he hasn't been seen!'

'Let's go and find him now,' Tumtum said. 'It's as good a time as any – the children will be at school, and Mr Mildew will be working.'

They set off at once, letting themselves out of the gates, then creeping underneath the dresser. But when they poked their noses out into the kitchen Arthur and Lucy were still there.

The Nutmouses waited while the children packed their satchels and buttoned their coats, before finally making to leave by the garden door.

'I wonder why she's taking oatcakes to school,' Nutmeg said, seeing the biscuit tin under Lucy's arm.

'Oh, I don't know, dear,' Tumtum replied, not thinking it of any significance.

As the children were going, Mr Mildew appeared in the kitchen. 'Have you remembered your captive?' he asked them.

'He's in here,' Lucy said, pointing to the tin. 'You do think he will be happy at school, don't you?'

'Oh, very happy. Very happy indeed,'

Mr Mildew mumbled, pouring cornflakes into his coffee cup. 'We certainly don't want him in the house, at any rate.'

The Nutmouses looked at each other in horror. 'Captive?' Nutmeg whispered. 'Surely they're not talking about the General?'

'I don't know but we'll soon find out!' Tumtum said.

When Mr Mildew's back was turned, they flew across the kitchen floor and raced up to the attic.

They realised at once that something was wrong – for there had been the most dreadful scuffle in the doll's house. The crockery was smashed, and all the furniture upturned, and two of the banister rails were broken.

'Look, the children have left us a letter,' Nutmeg said, pointing to the chest of drawers. The mice scrambled up to read it, dreading what it might say.

Dear Nutmeg,

We have found the elf and he's not really an elf at all. He's a mouse! But he is very sweet, and we like him. We have taken him to school in a biscuit tin, and he's going to live with the gerbils in Pets' House. He will be very happy there, because he'll have lots of friends to play with. And so now there won't be any more mess in the attic for you to clear up.

Love from,

Arthur and Lucy.

'He's been captured!' Nutmeg cried. 'Oh, how terrible! Just think of it! What will Mrs Marchmouse say? She'll be quite beside herself with grief. They may never see each other again! Oh, Tumtum, we have to save him!'

'We will, dear,' Tumtum said quietly. 'Now, come on! We must follow the children to school at once.'

Knowing there was not a moment to lose, they both hurtled downstairs to the kitchen, then slithered outside under the garden door. The mist was still clearing, and as they beat a path through the grass their coats got soaked in dew.

The school was just a few hundred yards or so from Rose Cottage, down the lane that led past

the village shop. The mice had often walked as far as the school gates, for they had friends who lived in a letterbox a little way beyond them. But in the past they had always made the journey at night, when there was no one about.

This morning it took them longer, for there were several people milling in the lane, and a cat prowling menacingly. So instead of going along the tarmac, they climbed up on to the bank and scrabbled along under cover of the hedgerow.

It took them nearly an hour to reach the school gates. The playground was deserted, for the children were already in assembly. So they ran straight towards the school building, then crawled inside through an air vent. They came out in the middle of a corridor full of bags and duffel coats.

It was a small school, but to the Nutmouses it seemed as big as a town. The children's wooden lockers were the size of houses, and the tiled corridor, lit by bright neon lights, stretched before them like a long road.

For a moment they felt quite dazed. 'Come on,' Tumtum said eventually, taking Nutmeg by the paw and pulling her across the corridor. 'Let's try in here.'

He led her under a door with 'Form 3A' written on it. On the other side, they found themselves in a room full of wooden desks, taller than Nutmouse Hall. 'How disgusting!' Nutmeg said, seeing a big glob of chewing gum stuck under one of the table tops.

The Nutmouses went all round the room,

shouting the General's name. But there was no squeak from him.

So they hurried back into the corridor, and tried the next door along.

This one had 'Form 2B' written on it, and as they wriggled underneath they became aware of some sort of commotion going on inside. At first they could just hear shouting and shrieking. But then, rising above the din, came the unmistakable voice of General Marchmouse.

'I'll have you know that I am an officer in the Royal Mouse Army, you little ruffians!' they heard him roar; then there was a chorus of jeers.

'That's him all right!' Tumtum said, as he and Nutmeg crept into the classroom. But what they saw gave them a horrible fright.

In the far corner of the room there was a big wire cage, standing on a table. And inside, the General was imprisoned with a crowd of naked gerbils.

The room was otherwise deserted, so the Nutmouses ran straight towards them. As they got closer, they could see that one of the gerbils was flicking the General with bits of straw. The cage was lined with filthy bedding and, to Nutmeg's horror, the food had been served in a communal trough.

The gerbils were making such a racket that the Nutmouses had to shout to get the General's attention.

'Oh, Mr and Mrs Nutmouse!' he cried, when he finally heard them calling up to him from the floor. 'Oh, thank heaven you've come! I have

been most hideously abused! I've not even a blazer to my name! Oh, the shame of it!'

'I want to take a look at the bars on your cage, General,' Tumtum shouted back. 'I might be able to cut through them with a hacksaw. But I can't climb the table – the legs are too slippery. Is there anything you can throw down?'

When they heard the word 'hacksaw', the gerbils fell silent.

They had lived all their lives in captivity, but they still hadn't given up hope of escape. And the thought of getting their paws on a hacksaw made their hearts tremble with excitement.

'Hold there, whoever you are!' one of them squeaked down to Tumtum. 'We'll make you a ladder.'

The gerbils all worked together, and in what seemed like no time they had plaited a sturdy ladder out of their filthy straw bedding. They tied one end of it to the bars of the cage, and tossed the other down to Tumtum and Nutmeg, who climbed it hurriedly. Tumtum went first, so he could help Nutmeg up on to the table top.

But when they reached the cage, they realised that the General's predicament was much worse than they had feared.

The cage bars were nearly a quarter of an inch thick; it would take the Nutmouses weeks to saw through them. And the door was secured with a padlock twenty times the size of the one they used on the gates of Nutmouse Hall. They would never be able to break it open.

The gerbils looked on intently as Tumtum and Nutmeg walked round and round their cage, looking for any possible escape routes. The General, who was usually so good in a crisis, was slumped miserably on the exercise wheel.

'I just can't understand it,' he moaned. 'This classroom is commanded by a teacher called Miss Short, and before she led her troops into assembly I told her who I was, and demanded in no uncertain terms that I be let out. But she ignored me! *She ignored me!* And all the children seemed to think it a great joke that I was wearing underpants. "A mouse in pants! A mouse in pants!" they all squealed, as though they expected me to be entirely naked! I have never felt so misunderstood.'

'Who keeps the key to this cage?' Tumtum asked, ignoring this self-pitying speech.

'The caretaker,' the General replied glumly.

'Where does he keep it?' Nutmeg enquired.

'On a big key ring round his belt,' the General said. 'He wears it at all times, except when he's opening the door. And he's a giant of a fellow. You haven't a hope of getting it off him.'

'And when does he open the door?' Tumtum persisted.

'During the lunch break, when everyone else is in the dining room,' piped up one of the gerbils, who had known the same routine all his life. 'But he only opens it for a few seconds – just long enough to stick his fist in, and dump more food in the trough.'

'And do the children ever take you out for exercise?' Nutmeg asked.

'Never!' another gerbil replied. 'Miss Short won't let them, because we give her the creeps – I've heard her say so. So the children just poke their fingers through the bars and tickle us. And when there's a special occasion – a parents' day or some such – they decorate us.'

'How?' Nutmeg asked, astonished.

'Oh, all sorts of things,' the gerbil prattled. 'Last time, they tied pink ribbons round our necks and –'

But at this disclosure he was interrupted by a great gulping sound. To everyone's astonishment, General Marchmouse was weeping.

'Oh, the shame!' he cried wretchedly. 'The

shame of it all! Can you imagine if *The Mouse Times* finds out about this! I can see their front page now: "General Marchmouse has been captured. He is imprisoned in a school cage, with a pink ribbon tied round his neck." I shall never live it down!'

Even the gerbils were touched by this, for there is something very upsetting about the sight of a grown mouse crying, no matter how badly he has behaved.

But try as they might, there was nothing anyone could say to console the General that morning.

Chapter Eight

The General was still sobbing when the mice heard the children making their way back from assembly.

'I'll think of something,' Tumtum promised him. Then he and Nutmeg fled back down the ladder.

As soon as they reached the floor, the gerbils hoisted it back up into the cage and hid it beneath their bedding. Then the door opened and Miss Short came in, followed by the children.

'Quick, this way!' Tumtum shouted, pulling his wife towards the wall. They ran along the skirting board, searching for somewhere to hide. But there was not a mouse hole to be found.

In desperation, they dived into a satchel lying open on the floor. Once they were inside, it felt oddly familiar. The canvas had been patched with gold thread, and there was a wooden pencil case with the initials 'A.M.' scratched into the lid.

'Why, it's Arthur's satchel!' Nutmeg exclaimed. 'I repaired it only last week. What luck, dear! This must be his classroom.'

'And we must be sitting under his desk,' Tumtum said.

The Nutmouses crouched at the bottom of the bag, among the crumbs and the sweet wrappers. All around, they could hear the sound of chairs and chattering voices. Then Miss Short clapped her hands, and the room fell silent.

'Now, class. I have an announcement to make,' she said.

Nutmeg wrinkled her nose. She didn't like the tone of Miss Short's voice.

'As you know, I have been wondering what to do about the gerbil problem,' Miss Short continued. 'When they came to live with us, there were only two gerbils. But now there are twelve! *Twelve gerbils*, children! Just think of it! If they continue to multiply at this rate, we shall have seventy-two gerbils by next term, and four hundred and thirty two gerbils by the term after that. And in a year, they will number *two thousand five hundred and ninety-two*!' (Miss Short was a maths teacher, so she enjoyed these sort of calculations.)

There were gasps all round the room, as these extraordinary statistics sank in.

'But two thousand five hundred and ninety-two gerbils wouldn't fit in the cage,' someone said.

'That is correct,' Miss Short replied. 'And it is for that reason that I have decided to find our gerbils a new home.'

There was a chorus of groans at this announcement, for the children had become quite attached to them. But Miss Short was adamant. 'Now don't be sad,' she said briskly. 'They will all be well looked after.'

'Where are they going, Miss Short?' someone asked. The Nutmouses, still hidden in Arthur's satchel, listened anxiously for her reply.

'I am happy to announce that they are going to a pet shop in town!' Miss Short said brightly, as though this was a special treat, like going to the cinema. 'I am going to take them there myself on Saturday, when I go to return my library books.'

'Will they be kept together?' one of the children asked.

The gerbils – who, like the Nutmouses, had been following every word – all held their breath.

Miss Short hesitated. Until that moment, she had not considered whether the gerbils would be kept together or not. She did not think it of any importance.

'I imagine they will be split into different cages, and sold in pairs,' she said finally. 'I doubt anyone would want to buy all of them together.'

The gerbils did not like the sound of this one little bit. When they heard that their family was to be separated they protested violently, hurling themselves against the bars, shouting and squawking and pleading for mercy.

'Dear me!' Miss Short said irritably. 'What a nasty noise they make. It's just as well we've found another home for them.'

'What will happen to the mouse?' someone asked. Tumtum and Nutmeg recognised the voice at once. It was Arthur's.

'The pet shop will find him a home too,' Miss Short replied. 'Perhaps they'll even find him a

mate. I'm sure there will be much demand for a mouse wearing underpants.'

The Nutmouses bristled with anger, willing Arthur to protest.

And he did, for Arthur wanted the General brought home too. It was *his* mouse, because it had been found in *his* cottage. It had been rather a nuisance there, it was true, and yet he felt protective towards it. And he didn't see why Miss Short thought she had the right to sell it.

'I can take him home with me again,' he said helpfully. 'He may as well go back where he came from.'

But Miss Short was not keen on this idea. 'Don't be silly, Arthur,' she replied. 'You told me yourself that you have no cage for it, and imagine what destruction it might cause if it were to run free. Just think – it might *multiply*.'

'But I want to take him home with me,' Arthur persisted. 'I wouldn't have brought him here if I'd thought he was going to be given away.'

'Now that's enough, Arthur,' Miss Short said crossly. 'These creatures are *all* going to the pet shop, and that is the last I am going to say on the matter.'

There was a sudden racket from the cage, as the General shouted something very rude at her – but Miss Short did not hear.

'Now, children,' she said briskly. 'Let's get out our maths books, shall we?' And though Arthur felt very indignant, he hesitated to say any more.

*

Tumtum and Nutmeg huddled in Arthur's satchel, their brains spinning. The town was ten miles away – if the General was taken there to be sold, he would never be seen again.

'We must think of something!' Nutmeg cried.

'We will, poppet,' Tumtum said, but he felt a deep foreboding. Saturday was the day after tomorrow – they had little time. He squeezed his wife's paw, trying not to show his fear.

'Oh, think, Tumtum! Think!' Nutmeg pleaded.

And think they did. There they sat in Arthur's satchel, thinking all through the maths lesson, then all through the English lesson too. And then they thought all through the spelling test; and when the bell rang for break they were still thinking so hard they both jumped. But they still hadn't thought of a plan.

They waited until the children had gone outside – less noisily than usual, for they were all subdued at the thought of losing their pets. Then, as soon as the room was quiet, the Nutmouses climbed out of the satchel and ran towards the cage.

The gerbils tossed down the ladder, and as soon as Tumtum and Nutmeg appeared they all threw themselves against the bars, clamouring for help.

'Do something, Mr and Mrs Nutmouse!' they cried. 'If they split us up our whole family will be destroyed. We'll never see each other again. You must help us. You're our only hope!'

Tumtum and Nutmeg tried to reassure them, but the situation was very bleak. The only consolation was that the General appeared to be back to his old self again. He had stopped his boo-hooing, and instead was standing with one foot on the feeding trough, spitting with rage.

'A pet shop!' he fumed. 'A pet shop! How dare that wretched woman presume to dispatch the great General Marchmouse to a pet shop!'

Tumtum turned to him, as a sudden inspiration struck. 'Do you think it might be worth calling in the Royal Mouse Army, General?' he asked. 'They could launch an attack on the caretaker next time he opens the cage.'

The gerbils all pricked up their ears at the mention of the Royal Mouse Army — but the General was dismissive.

'Pah! Do you imagine I hadn't thought of that already?' he snorted. 'I am confident, of course, that the Royal Mouse Army would send every soldier it could muster to rescue *me*. But there's no point trying to summon it. All the troops are undergoing a week's intensive pogo-training at Apple Farm — it's nearly two miles away, they'd never get back here in time.

'And besides,' he went on, 'there's nothing the army could do against the caretaker. He's huge — if you fired a cannonball at him, he wouldn't even feel it.' (This was probably true, for the Royal Mouse Army's cannonballs were the size of raisins.)

As this one ray of hope was extinguished, the gerbils looked even more wretched. Some were hugging each other now and sobbing, dreading the parting to come.

Meanwhile, Tumtum and Nutmeg went on thinking. But even after thinking for another three whole minutes, which is a long time in a mouse's life, they still hadn't thought what to do.

Chapter Nine

Eventually, just as Nutmeg was thinking she could think no more, an extraordinary idea began to play itself out in her mind. She squeezed her eyes tight shut, feeling a shiver run down her spine.

'I've had a brainwave!' she announced.

'What is it, dear?' Tumtum asked eagerly. Nutmeg's brainwaves were not always sensible, but they were often spectacular. And he felt they were all in need of something spectacular just now.

'We must summon Miss Tiptoe's ballet school!' Nutmeg said.

Everyone looked bewildered. They had all heard of Miss Tiptoe's ballet school, of course, for it was the most famous ballet school in the land. It was situated in the church vestry, and smart young mice came from far and wide to board there for a term or two. If you went to a mouse ball you could always tell the mice who had been trained by Miss Tiptoe, because they moved round the dance floor much more gracefully than anyone else.

But what possible use could Miss Tiptoe and her ballerinas be against the giant caretaker?

'*The ballet school*, Mrs Nutmouse?' the

General said witheringly. 'I suppose this is your idea of a joke.'

'Oh no, General. I wouldn't joke at a time like this,' Nutmeg replied excitedly. 'Our only hope of setting you all free is to get hold of the key to the padlock. But Tumtum and I can't do that if the caretaker's wearing the key ring on his belt –'

'Yes, yes,' the General interrupted. 'So how will your dancers save the day?'

'Just listen,' Nutmeg said impatiently. 'You said that the caretaker removes the key ring in order to open the padlock – so that's when we must snatch it. But Tumtum and I could never do it alone; we wouldn't be strong enough. And even if we managed to tug it from the caretaker's hands, he'd catch us before we could run away with it.

'But imagine if Miss Tiptoe's ballerinas were assembled in the wings, hiding behind a desk, or a waste paper basket . . . and imagine if each ballerina was mounted on a pogo stick, waiting until the caretaker came to unlock the cage. And then imagine if they all bounced silently towards him on their sticks, bouncing higher and higher, until they were bouncing so high that they could snatch the keys from his hands, and bounce away with them! I've seen Miss Tiptoe's ballerinas performing in the church, and they're so nimble and light-footed that the caretaker would hardly know what had happened until it was all over!'

Everyone looked stunned. Nutmeg's proposal was so extraordinary that it took a while for it to sink in. They tried to picture the incredible scene she had described. A troupe of tiny ballerinas, ambushing the colossal caretaker! Could it really work?

The gerbils weren't at all sure. But they *had* to believe in it. It was their only hope.

'I think it's a splendid plan!' one of them declared. 'Quite splendid! Quite ingenious! I wish I'd thought of it myself!'

This was all the encouragement the other gerbils needed. With a great roar of approval they rose to their feet and started cheering, 'Hooray for Mrs Nutmouse!' Tumtum clapped his wife on the back, feeling very proud.

But the General still looked scornful. 'If the caretaker's keys were snatched, he'd run after

them,' he said. 'The ballerinas wouldn't stand a chance.'

'You underestimate them, General,' Nutmeg said. 'Miss Tiptoe's mice are the nimblest in England. They're so light, they can almost fly. When they've snatched the key ring, they'll drag it into the corner of the room before the caretaker's recovered his wits. Tumtum and I will be waiting for them, and we can unhook the key to the cage.'

'He's got hundreds of keys on his belt. How will you know which it is?' the General asked.

'It's the small green one,' one of the gerbils replied. 'He paints his keys different colours so he can tell one from the other.'

'Good – and when we've removed it, we'll tie the key ring to the girls' pogo sticks,' Nutmeg went on eagerly. 'Then the entire dance troupe will bounce out into the corridor, with the bunch of keys clattering behind them. While the caretaker runs after them, Tumtum and I will climb up the ladder and unlock the cage.'

'But what if the caretaker catches the ballerinas?' Tumtum asked, voicing everyone's worst fear.

'He won't,' Nutmeg answered firmly. 'They will move much too fast for him, especially if they're on pogo sticks. As soon as we've opened the cage, we'll sound the all-clear. Then the ballerinas can simply drop the keys and bounce back into the playground through the air vent.'

'Where do you intend to get hold of the pogo sticks?' the General asked, determined to find some hitch in Nutmeg's plan.

'You said that the Royal Mouse Army had a big supply of them – we'll borrow some from the barracks,' she replied. 'Surely they're unlikely to refuse if you write us a letter of authorisation.'

The General considered all this for a moment, stroking his whiskers. He supposed it might just work; and it was certainly better than having no plan at all. And yet something about it made him uneasy. The truth was that his pride had been deeply wounded by his imprisonment, and the thought of being rescued by ballerinas was more than he could bear. Imagine if one of the gerbils sneaked about it to the village – he'd be a laughing stock!

But, as he mulled things over, a more cheerful

picture began to appear.

Perhaps it needn't be so humiliating, so long as I take sole command, he mused. *I might be behind bars, but I can still issue orders, and I can still take all the credit if it works. Why! This could turn out to be one of my greatest battles yet!*

The General felt a quiet flutter in his stomach. How impressed everyone would be if he won! In his mind's eye, he could already see his picture on the front page of *The Mouse Times*, accompanied by a glorious report: 'The Great General Marchmouse conquers against all odds.He escapes, Houdini style, from a gerbils' cage, and sends a giant school caretaker fleeing for his life.'

The involvement of Miss Tiptoe's ballerinas

could be glossed over entirely.

'How soon can the dancers be mobilised?' he asked.

'We shall have to find out,' Tumtum replied, relieved that his wife's plan had been accepted. 'Nutmeg and I have got a lot to do. First we must get to the barracks and collect the pogo sticks. Then we'll go and see Miss Tiptoe, and persuade her to lend us her dancers. And that mightn't be easy – it's a risky enterprise, and she'll probably have grave misgivings about them taking part.'

'Not when she learns that it is *my* freedom that's at stake,' the General said grandly.

Tumtum ignored this, and looked at his watch. It was nearly twenty past eleven; the children would be returning from break at any moment. 'We must go at once,' he said, turning to his wife.

The Nutmouses quickly shimmied down to the floor. And just as the gerbils were whisking the ladder back into the cage, the door burst open and the members of Form 2B started pouring into the room.

'We'll be back tonight!' Tumtum called over his shoulder, as he and Nutmeg hurtled under a filing cabinet. They waited until the children were all seated, and had their heads in their books. Then they crept out under the door, and across the corridor towards the air vent.

'Bring me my field glasses and my compass and my pistol and my whisky flask and my military

uniform and something decent to eat!' the General called after them — but the Nutmouses were already gone.

Chapter Ten

The General would have been tickled to know that Arthur and Lucy had spent the whole of break time thinking about him. As soon as the bell went, Arthur had rushed into the playground to find his sister, and tell her all about Miss Short's plans. As he had expected, Lucy thought it all just as unfair as he did.

'It's bad enough her selling the gerbils, but

she's got no right to sell *our* mouse!' she said crossly. 'We brought him here thinking he would have a happy home. But if he goes to the pet shop he might end up with someone horrible – someone who forgets to feed him.'

When they had found the mouse in the doll's house, they had not felt nearly as protective of him as they did now. They had just been annoyed that he had made so much mess, and that he had eaten Nutmeg's tea.

But when they had seen him looking so unhappy in the gerbils' cage they had felt a pang of remorse, thinking it might have been kinder to have kept him at Rose Cottage. And now that he was to be sent away forever, they felt even worse.

'What will happen if he goes to the pet shop

and no one buys him?' Arthur asked.

'I suppose he might be put down,' Lucy said glumly.

'*Put down?*' Arthur whispered, not liking the sound of this. 'What do you mean, put down?'

'Oh, I don't know,' Lucy replied, not wanting to upset him further. 'I just mean we must rescue him before something awful happens.'

'How can we rescue him if we can't open the cage?' Arthur asked. 'The caretaker's got the keys.'

'Well, we can just ask him to open it, then,' Lucy said, not knowing what else to suggest.

'But he won't,' Arthur said. And Lucy suspected he was right, for the caretaker was not very friendly.

'Well, we should tell Nutmeg then,' Lucy

said. 'And ask her to come to school and rescue him for us.'

'Do you think she'd come all this way?' Arthur asked doubtfully. Somehow he didn't like the idea of Nutmeg coming to his school. She was their secret, and he felt they should keep her to themselves.

'Of course she would,' Lucy said confidently. 'The school's not far from Rose Cottage, after all, and she can come at night when there's no one here.'

'I suppose so,' Arthur said. But he still felt uneasy.

Later that day, before going to bed, he and Lucy sat down and wrote a long letter to Nutmeg, telling her all about Miss Short's plan to sell their mouse, and asking her to return him to Rose Cottage.

. . . If you bring him home again we'll find him a nice big bucket to live in, and we'll let him out for runs in the bath. We'd look after him very well, they concluded.

Meanwhile, Nutmeg's day had been most eventful. After leaving the school, she and Tumtum had made straight for the Royal Mouse Army's barracks to see if they could borrow some pogo sticks. They needed thirteen, for Miss Tiptoe always had thirteen ballerinas in her school. It was something she was very particular about.

The barracks were on the other side of the village green, in a dugout underneath the war memorial. It had formerly been a fox's lair, but the Royal Mouse Army had taken it over some years ago, and now it was a warren of underground dormitories and ammunition stores.

Tumtum and Nutmeg arrived at the main entrance to find two sentries playing poker. When Tumtum showed them General Marchmouse's letter, requesting that the pogo sticks be released immediately, they were not at all helpful.

One said that all the pogo sticks were locked in a store room, and that he didn't know where to find the key. The other said he thought he might know where the key was, but that he couldn't go and look for it because he had a sprained ankle. And then the other one said he had a sprained ankle too, at which both sentries started cackling.

Tumtum became exasperated. 'Now look here,' he said crossly. 'I happen to be on lunching terms with your commanding officer, Brigadier Flashmouse and –'

Suddenly, both the sentries became more cooperative. One offered Tumtum a slug of whiskey from his hip flask, while the other went inside and returned with thirteen pogo sticks, each with the Royal Mouse Army's initials, R.M.A, engraved near the tip. Tumtum signed for them, then the Nutmouses hurried on their way.

They made straight for the ballet school, crossing the lane at the top of the green, then climbing up the steep verge that led into the church yard.

'Hang on!' Tumtum said, suddenly noticing three women coming up the church path with bundles of flowers. He and Nutmeg waited until they had gone into the porch, then followed behind.

There were more women inside the church, arranging big bouquets of lilies. But they were concentrating much too hard on their work to notice two mice scuttling down the aisle towards the vestry.

The entrance to Miss Tiptoe's school was through a little mouse hole, hidden behind an old oak chest. There was no door, just a frayed velvet curtain to keep out the draft. The Nutmouses dumped the pogo sticks on the floor and went inside.

The school was in a big, chilly cupboard with dark red walls and a flagstone floor. Long ago, it was where all the church silver had been kept. But then the silver had been sold and the cupboard wasn't needed any more. So Miss Tiptoe had taken it over.

The school was lit by candles borrowed from the church and it took a moment or two for Tumtum and Nutmeg's eyes to become accustomed to the dim flickering light.

They could just make out the ballerinas in the far corner, practising at the bar. All thirteen of them were present, dressed in white tutus with gold braids in their hair. Miss Tiptoe was sitting next to them at the piano, playing soft, tinkling tunes. Tumtum knew the piano well – it had once lived in the drawing room of Nutmouse Hall, but he had given it to Miss Tiptoe when her last piano had got dry rot. (Miss Tiptoe's pianos often got dry rot, for the cupboard was rather damp.)

The Nutmouses waited until Miss Tiptoe had finished playing before approaching her. She was surprised to see them, for mice seldom visited her school unannounced. But their expressions clearly told her that something was wrong.

'Carry on practising, girls,' she instructed her class. Then she got up and led the Nutmouses to her desk, which stood in a corner of the cupboard, raised on a red hymn book. She walked with a stick, but her back was as straight as a ruler. She sat on a big throne-like chair, while the Nutmouses

faced her perched on tiny embroidered footstools.

Miss Tiptoe was very beautiful and composed, and everyone found her a little intimidating. She was tall and thin and grey – and astonishingly old. No one knew how old, but one of Nutmeg's sisters had been taught by her when she was a young girl, and she had seemed very old then. And now of course she was even older.

She listened silently while Tumtum told her all about the General's capture, and explained the amazing role they hoped her ballerinas might play in his and the gerbils' release.

The Nutmouses had expected that she might be shocked at their request, but she had a calm, wise expression on her face. Miss Tiptoe had seen many odd things in her life, and she knew the strange and wonderful plots of all the classical ballets, so it took a lot to surprise her.

'I'm . . . er, I'm sure your ballerinas would look most elegant on pogo sticks, Miss Tiptoe,' Tumtum concluded, feeling rather awkward.

Miss Tiptoe looked at him piercingly. 'Imagine that you were in my position, Mr Nutmouse,' she said, speaking in a very clear voice. 'Would you risk your pupils' lives for the sake of the General?'

Tumtum said nothing, but his silence was as good an answer as any. For of course, he knew that if he had a daughter he wouldn't want her risking her life on account of anyone.

Miss Tiptoe's expression softened. 'Is the General a close friend of yours, Mr Nutmouse?'

she asked kindly.

'I suppose he is,' Tumtum replied. 'I know he can be exasperating, and a bit above himself, but there is a side to him which is good and loyal too. And he is a great hero, of course.'

Miss Tiptoe nodded. She did not know the General well, but like all the mice in the village she felt a certain loyalty to him. For whenever there had been trouble, such as when rats had invaded the village grain store, he and his troops had always risen to save the day. It would seem a terrible comedown if he were to end his days in a pet shop.

She looked pensive a moment, for she was still wavering. But her conscience told her what to do. 'Bring your pogo sticks inside, Mr Nutmouse,' she said calmly. 'My ballerinas will do what is required of them.'

Tumtum and Nutmeg both let out a cry of relief.

'Oh, thank you, Miss Tiptoe! Thank you!' Nutmeg gulped, leaping up to embrace her.

But by the time Nutmeg had found her feet, Miss Tiptoe had already glided back to her pupils. 'Come along now, girls!' she cried, rapping her stick on the floor. 'We have a new routine to rehearse!'

Chapter Eleven

None of the ballerinas had used a pogo stick before, but they took to them at once, leaping into the air as gracefully as gazelles with Miss Tiptoe accompanying them on the piano. Before long, they were bouncing so high they could touch the cupboard ceiling.

When she felt they could bounce no better, Miss Tiptoe sent the girls off to have tea, which was

148

served next door, in a flour bin in the vicarage kitchen.

'Oh, Miss Tiptoe! They were splendid!' cried Nutmeg, who had been watching spellbound. Miss Tiptoe smiled graciously. Then she listened as Tumtum spelled out the plan of attack.

'We'll come back early in the morning, and escort you and your girls to Form 2B before the school opens,' he began. 'That way you can familiarise yourselves with the classroom, and take instructions from the General before any of the children turn up. Then you can find somewhere to hide away until the caretaker comes on his lunchtime rounds. It will be a long wait, but it's important that all the dancers are out of sight before school begins.'

Miss Tiptoe raised her eyes when Tumtum mentioned taking instructions from the General. But she made no comment.

'I will entrust you with the refreshments, Mrs Nutmouse,' was all she said. 'If my girls are to spend all morning cooped up underneath a filing cabinet, they will need something to nibble.'

'Of course,' Nutmeg replied eagerly, and she at once began planning a sumptuous picnic.

By the time the Nutmouses left the vestry, the flower-arrangers had long gone. The lights had been turned off, and the church was almost dark. As they walked back down the aisle hand in hand, they heard the clock strike five.

'Five o'clock, Tumtum!' Nutmeg sighed. 'And we've so much to do. I've to prepare the

picnic, and then we'll have to go back to the school and tell the General what's happening and —'

'There is no need to go back to the school tonight,' Tumtum said firmly. 'We've a busy day tomorrow, and we must go home and rest. We'll see the General first thing in the morning.'

The thought of rest was very tempting to Nutmeg, for all the excitement was beginning to take its toll on her. Her eyes felt heavy, and her ankles were starting to ache. As they walked home to Nutmouse Hall, she leaned wearily on Tumtum's shoulder.

They had only been away for a day, and yet the house had a deserted feel to it. The big rooms seemed empty and echoey now that the General had gone.

Nutmeg felt quite forlorn as she set about in the kitchen making a meatloaf and a mushroom quiche and a salmon mousse and a lemon cheesecake and two dozen jam tarts for the ballerinas.

While she worked, Tumtum put his feet up in the library. He felt forlorn too.

Much later, they sat down together to supper in the kitchen.

'What if our plan doesn't work?' Nutmeg said anxiously.

'It will work, dear,' Tumtum replied reassuringly. 'You saw how high those ballerinas could hop on their pogo sticks. They'll have no difficulty bouncing up and snatching the caretaker's keys.'

'But what if he catches them?' Nutmeg

fretted. 'Oh, those poor young girls. If he were to hurt them, I'd never forgive myself!'

'Now don't fuss, dear,' Tumtum said. 'They'll be bouncing so fast the caretaker won't even see them coming.'

'I do hope you're right,' Nutmeg said. But she could feel a dread rising in her stomach.

It had been her idea to enlist the help of the ballet school, and it had seemed such a splendid idea at first. And yet as the time of the rescue operation drew nearer, she had a horrible feeling that something was to go wrong.

Perhaps the General was right, she thought. *Perhaps the ballerinas simply aren't up to it.*

Nutmeg worried all through supper; and then she worried while she washed up; and she was still worrying when she and Tumtum sat down in the library to drink their cocoa. She knew she would never get to sleep, so she decided to go and tidy Arthur and Lucy's bedroom.

'I don't want them thinking I'm neglecting them, and this morning I noticed that Lucy's jersey needs darning,' she said when Tumtum protested. 'And I still haven't cleared up all the mess the General made in the doll's house.'

'Very well, dear, but don't be long,' Tumtum said, stifling a yawn. 'We both need an early night, and you've already done quite enough bustling for one day.'

But when Nutmeg reached the attic, she found the children's letter. And that made her even more anxious. For even if she managed to get the

General back from the school, she knew she couldn't possibly let Arthur and Lucy keep him in a bucket. He wouldn't like that at all.

She sat a long while at her desk in the doll's house, nibbling the end of her fountain pen and wondering how best to reply. The letter she finally wrote went as follows:

Dear Arthur and Lucy,

I intend to rescue your mouse tomorrow. This will be a very difficult mission, and I cannot guarantee that I will succeed. But if I do, perhaps it would be best if we were to set him free again. For I happen to know the mouse in question, and I doubt he would much enjoy living in a bucket.

Love,

Nutmeg.

Then, while the children slept, she darned the elbow of Lucy's jersey, and the toe of one of Arthur's socks, and she scrubbed the doll's house kitchen, and put all the furniture back to rights in the drawing room. And finally, feeling more tired than she could ever remember, she limped back to Nutmouse Hall and collapsed beside Tumtum in their four-poster bed.

Everyone in Rose Cottage slept soundly that night. But there was no such peace for the General. After the Nutmouses had left him, his day had gone from bad to worse.

After break, there had been a nature lesson, conducted by a gangly teacher called Mr Greaves, who had asked the class questions such as what field mice do in winter, and where squirrels sleep at night. The General had shouted all the answers loud and clear from his cage, but the teacher had ignored him.

Then there had been a maths lesson during which the children had recited their times tables. The gerbils turned out to know them all perfectly. But when the General tried to join in he'd got in the most dreadful muddle, and said that three times three was thirty-three, and that six times six was sixty-six. And then his cell mates had mocked him all the more.

By the time the children filed off for lunch, the General was feeling more homesick than he'd ever felt before. Even when he had been away at war for whole days on end, he had never felt as homesick as this. Then the caretaker had turned up to give the prisoners more revolting seeds to eat, and the General had felt sicker still.

For there was something off-putting about the caretaker. He was so tall he had to stoop almost double to open the door of the cage. And his fist was so wide that when he reached inside to dump the food in the feeding trough, the animals had to press themselves back against the bars so as not to be crushed. He was a curious-looking man too, with thick tufts of black hair coming from his nostrils, and red veins in his cheeks.

The General made clear his displeasure at the meal being served. 'Take away this filthy bird seed and bring me some decent roast beef!' he shouted. But the caretaker just slammed the cage door shut on him.

'How can you digest that muck?' the General asked sullenly, watching the gerbils crowd round the trough. But it had been a whole day since they had last eaten, and the gerbils' mouths were too full to reply.

As the afternoon wore on, with a history lesson followed by a spelling test (to which the gerbils recited all the correct answers, and he all the wrong ones), the General began to feel more and more wretched. And then a new crisis arose.

Shortly after the children had gone home, the caretaker appeared at the door of Form 2B. He found Miss Short in the room, tidying her desk.

'Can I lock up in here now?' he asked her.

'Yes, I'm just going. And I'll be taking these

beastly things with me,' she said, nodding towards the cage. 'I was going to get rid of them on Saturday, but I'm seeing my sister in town tonight so I might as well take them now.'

'What'll you do with them?' the caretaker asked casually.

'I'll take them to the pet shop,' she replied.

'I wouldn't do that,' he said. 'I know old Mr Dye who runs it, and he won't be wanting a cageful of flea-bitten old rodents like this. He sells fancy things – carp and budgies and the like.'

Miss Short sucked in her breath. 'Well, if the pet shop can't take them, I'll have to think again,' she said crisply. 'I'm sure the vet could dispose of them for me.'

At this the gerbils let out a collective cry of

horror, and started scrabbling frantically, desperate to get out. The General rattled the bars, swearing furiously at his captors. Then the floor lurched beneath their feet, as the cage was hoisted into the air.

Chapter Twelve

Tumtum and Nutmeg set out early next morning to collect the ballerinas. The milkman had not yet stirred, and the church spire was still shrouded in mist.

When they arrived in the vestry, they found Miss Tiptoe and her class waiting for them outside the cupboard. The girls were dressed in beige tutus, which had their names embroidered on them in silver thread. The Nutmouses studied them a moment, so that they might remember who was who. There was Trixibelle, who had the long, beautiful ears . . . There was Millicent Millybobbette, who was the shortest . . . There was Lillyloop, who was the tallest . . . There was Horseradish, with the pink braids in her tail . . . and Tartare, with the sharp, silver toenails —

But it was no good. They could never remember so many names; just trying made their heads spin. And they were such odd names too. In their day mice had been given simple names, like Nutmeg.

'You told me that the school had wooden floors, so I decided beige would be our best disguise,' Miss Tiptoe said. She had been up all

night sewing.

'How clever of you,' Nutmeg replied. She suddenly felt embarrassed by the bright green cape she was wearing, and wished she had dressed more discreetly.

Presently, the party set forth. They were a curious convoy, with the girls bouncing along like crickets on their pogo sticks, and Miss Tiptoe gliding elegantly beside them, while Tumtum and Nutmeg straggled in the rear with the picnic baskets.

The girls were in high spirits, and Horseradish shrieked when Tartare tried to bounce away with her earmuffs.

'Young ladies! Please recall that you are representing the ballet school!' Miss Tiptoe said sharply, and then they all looked a little chastened.

Before long they reached the school gates and saw the tarmac playground stretching before them. The girls all craned their necks as they looked up at the vast steel climbing frame. To them, it seemed as tall as a skyscraper.

'This way,' said Tumtum, leading the party towards the air vent. He pushed the pogo sticks through the grille first, then the mice climbed inside.

The ballerinas had never been in a school for human children, and the building felt cold and unfamiliar. They found something ominous about the huge shoes in the lockers and the enormous overalls hanging from the pegs on the wall. It was all so different to their own little school in the vestry.

They kept close together as they followed Tumtum under the door of Form 2B. It was dark, for the blinds were shut, and they couldn't see as far as the cage. Everything was deathly quiet. 'The prisoners must still be asleep,' Tumtum said, leading his party across the room.

'General! Gerbils! We're back!' he called up from beneath the table. 'Throw down the ladder!'

But there wasn't a sound.

He called again, wondering why they didn't reply. Then, blinking, Nutmeg let out a cry: 'The cage! It's gone!'

The Nutmouses stood motionless, stunned by this discovery. They couldn't understand it. Miss Short had said that she was taking the gerbils to the pet shop on Saturday, but Saturday wasn't until tomorrow.

'The cage must have been moved to another part of the school,' Tumtum said urgently. 'We'll search all the classrooms. Miss Tiptoe – you and your girls head down the corridor to your left, and look under every door. We'll try the rooms to the right.'

The mice hurtled back out of Form 2B, and dispersed down the corridor, shouting the General's name. Miss Tiptoe's ballerinas bounced high and low around the gymnasium, and the art room, and the kitchen. And the Nutmouses scuttled round Form 3A, and Form 1C, and all round the staff room, and the music room – but the cage was nowhere to be seen.

'He must have gone to the pet shop!' Nutmeg wailed. She had a sudden vision of Mrs Marchmouse living the rest of her life alone in the big, rackety gun cupboard with no one to keep her company – and she started to weep.

'I will take my girls back to the vestry, since it seems there is no use for us here,' Miss Tiptoe said tactfully.

The subdued rescue party made its way back down the corridor towards the air vent. The girls walked quietly, pulling their pogo sticks behind them. None of them had met the General before, but the thought of any mouse being taken to a pet shop was enough to take all the bounce out of them.

But just as they were about to climb back outside, Tumtum suddenly stopped in his tracks. 'What's that?' he said, motioning the party to be still. They all stood quivering, their ears pricked. They could hear faint squeals.

'Over there! They're in there!' Tumtum cried, pointing to the cupboard door across the corridor. Miss Tiptoe's dancers had passed it by – they'd looked in all the classrooms, but they hadn't thought of exploring the cupboards too.

As Tumtum wriggled under the door, he could hear the gerbils howling. And rising above them was the voice of a most indignant General Marchmouse: 'We're here, you fools! Let us out! LET US OUT!'

'Where?' Tumtum shouted, fumbling for his

torch. 'It's pitch black. I can't see a thing.'

'Here!' squeaked a dozen voices. 'HERE!'

'Where?' Tumtum called again, flashing his torch about.

'*Up here!*' they chorused impatiently.

Tumtum craned his neck and shone his torch back and forth along the shelves. At first all he could see were cardboard boxes.

But then, on the lowest shelf, he noticed a big lump, covered with a filthy grey blanket. He shone his torch over it, trying to make out what it was. All of a sudden, the corner of the blanket tweaked, and the straw ladder came tumbling to the floor.

'Quick! I've found them,' Tumtum shouted under the door. The rest of the mice raced after him and they all clambered up to the prisoners.

'Uncover us!' the General shouted furiously; and with the Nutmouses and Miss Tiptoe and the thirteen ballerinas pulling and tugging as one, they eventually managed to drag the blanket from the cage.

When Tumtum shone his torch on the prisoners, it was clear that there had been quite a commotion. The exercise wheel had been snapped in two, and everyone was badly bruised. The General had a black eye, and was in an especially ill humour.

'Why the devil didn't you come back last night?' he asked furiously. 'We've been sentenced to death, every last one of us!'

Each prisoner had a different version of what

had happened, and everyone talked at once, so the story was rather hard to follow.

But it seemed that after Miss Short's threat to transport them all to the pet shop, the General had become quite wild with anger. And when she'd picked up the cage he'd sunk his teeth deep into her finger – drawing blood, or biting it right off, depending whose account you believed.

Miss Short had then dropped the cage on the floor, and it had landed with a great crash, which is what had caused all the cuts and bruises and black eyes. She had shrieked a good deal, using words which had made the lady gerbils cover their ears – but the upshot was that she was too frightened to go near the cage again. And she had told the caretaker that she would not take it in her car, nor did she want it to remain in Form 2B.

So the caretaker had offered to get rid of it, saying that he would dispose of the gerbils at the weekend. Miss Short had not enquired how he intended to do this, but he had muttered something about having a friend who kept owls – and that had made all the prisoners quake, for they knew that owls liked nothing more than a succulent little mouse or gerbil to nibble.

And then the caretaker had dumped them in the dark cupboard, out of Miss Short's sight. He had thrown the blanket over them in order to muffle their protests, and left them to await their terrifying fate.

'The worst of it was thinking you'd never find

us, Mrs Nutmouse,' one of the gerbils said pitifully.

Nutmeg said nothing. For she feared that her plan might no longer work. It wouldn't be nearly so easy now that the cage was in a cupboard instead of in the classroom. And besides, the caretaker's routine might have changed. There was no knowing what time he'd come and feed the gerbils now – or if he would come at all.

'Our plan will still succeed so long as everyone follows my commands to the letter,' the General said bossily, reading her thoughts. Then he looked at Tumtum, and started giving orders.

'You and all the dancers must hide on the other side of the corridor, under the shoe lockers, until the caretaker comes to feed us,' he said. 'When he opens the door and removes the keys from his belt, I'll give the order to hop. But nobody is to move until I issue it!'

'When do you think the caretaker will come?' Tumtum asked.

'Oh, I don't know!' the General snapped. 'But if he wants to feed us to the owls, then it's in his interest to fatten us up. I should think he'll come soon enough.'

'Very good, General,' Tumtum said, looking at his watch. 'We'd better hurry up and hide. It's nearly eight o'clock and the school will be opening soon.'

'We're starving!' one of the gerbils cried. 'Did you bring us anything to eat?'

'Oh, I don't think you'll be short of things to eat,' Tumtum said, shining his torch over the labels on the cardboard boxes. 'You've been locked up in the tuck shop!'

Chapter Thirteen

There was a great whoop of joy from the gerbils when they read the words on the boxes. They had been locked away with a lifetime's supply of walnut whips, and fudge bars, and sherbet dips, and potato crisps! Even the General managed a cheer when he saw the enormous carton of humbugs.

The Nutmouses spent a frantic few minutes

nibbling through all the cardboard packaging, and distributing the food. Tumtum pulled out a bar of hazelnut chocolate, and passed chunks into the cage; then he wrestled the cap off a tube of Smarties and showered them down on to the prisoners. Nutmeg handed them crisps and wine gums, and long strands of strawberry liquorice.

The ballerinas were looking longingly at a box of jelly beans, for it seemed an eternity since breakfast. But Miss Tiptoe did not approve of sweets and promptly shooed them all back down the ladder.

When the prisoners had been given all they could eat, the Nutmouses scurried down after the others. Then the mice lay in wait on the other side of the corridor, beneath the long row of lockers.

A few moments later, a bright light came on, and they felt the floor quake as the children charged into the building. The ballerinas huddled together, watching the huge feet thundering by. One of the children stopped just in front of them to hang up her coat, and the tips of her shoes poked under the locker, brushing Horseradish's tutu. Then suddenly a bell clanged, and the children disappeared into their classrooms.

After that, the mice had a long, anxious wait for the caretaker to appear. The hideaway was cramped and dusty, and had it not been for their picnic they would have felt very glum.

Arthur was having an uneasy time too. The moment he had walked into Form 2B, he had noticed the empty table where the cage had been, and had felt a sense of foreboding.

'Where are the gerbils?' he asked Miss Short, who was sitting at her desk eating a marmalade sandwich.

'I will explain to you when we are all sitting down,' she replied annoyingly.

It seemed a very long wait until everyone had settled, and Miss Short had gone through the register.

'Now, children,' she said eventually, speaking with forced cheerfulness. 'Some of you may have noticed that our large family of gerbils is no longer with us.'

'Where have they gone?' they all cried.

'They have been *removed*,' Miss Short replied.

She spoke as though referring to something distasteful, like a rotten egg. 'And I will tell you why,' she continued, raising her voice as the children bombarded her with more questions. 'Last night, I learned that our gerbils were not the timid creatures we assumed them to be . . . One of them bit me!'

Miss Short paused a moment, while this information sank in. To force the point, she raised the first finger of her left hand, to show off a small strip of sticking plaster.

'How come?' Arthur asked suspiciously, for he knew that Miss Short never went near the cage.

'It bit me when I tried to give it something nice to eat,' Miss Short lied. 'And when I discovered how dangerous the little creatures were, I knew I must remove them at once, for we wouldn't want any of you being injured, would we? I didn't dare put the cage in my car, so the caretaker kindly agreed to deliver the animals to the pet shop for me.'

'Has he taken them already?' Arthur asked anxiously.

'I sincerely hope so,' Miss Short said. 'I have told him that I do not wish to see them inside the school building *ever again*.'

The children were shocked by this development, and they felt that the story didn't quite add up. But when they pressed Miss Short for more information she got very cross and told them that she never wanted to hear any mention of the beastly gerbils again.

Arthur was so upset he couldn't concentrate on any of his lessons. Then at break time he rushed to find Lucy in the playground to tell her what had happened. 'So she *hopes* the caretaker's already taken them, but she didn't say he definitely had,' he explained.

'But he must have done,' Lucy said miserably. 'They're not in any of the classrooms, and they can't be in the staffroom because Miss Short said she didn't want to see them again.'

The children sat down together on the bench beside the netball court, feeling wretched. They wished they had never brought their mouse to school.

'We could go to the town, and find the pet shop, and *buy* him back,' Arthur suggested. But even as he said it, he knew it wouldn't work. For the town was ten miles away, and their father had no car to take them there. Besides which, they had only eighty-eight pence between them, and a mouse would surely cost more than that.

They felt so cast down that it was almost a relief when the bell rang to mark the end of break.

But as they were making their way back inside, they saw the caretaker walking towards them. He had come from the direction of the shed in the corner of the playground where he kept all his things. He was carrying a brown sack.

'That's the gerbils' food,' Arthur said in surprise. 'I've seen him with it before. Come on, let's follow him and see where he goes.'

The children waited until he had gone

inside, then crept after him down the corridor. But halfway along it, he disappeared into the boiler room.

'Surely he can't be feeding the gerbils in *there*?' Lucy said, thinking it a very odd place to hide them.

They waited outside, pretending to be looking for something in one of the lockers. They should have been back in their classrooms by now, but they had to see what happened.

Presently, the caretaker reappeared, still carrying the brown sack. The children watched, motionless, as he walked on down the corridor, then stopped outside the tuck cupboard. He stood there a moment, glancing left and right. He looked nervous, as if he didn't want anyone to see what he

was doing. Then he removed the keys from his belt, and opened the cupboard door.

As he did so, the Nutmouses and Miss Tiptoe hovered at the rim of the locker, watching his every move. The ballerinas were lined up behind them, mounted on their pogo sticks, poised to advance the moment the General gave the order.

'On your marks, girls!' they heard him bellow from inside the cage. 'Get set . . . CHARGE!'

But just as the order was given, Nutmeg issued a counter command. 'STOP! STOP!' she shrieked, pointing down the corridor. 'Tumtum, look! It's Arthur and Lucy! We can't let them see us!'

'Hold back, girls!' Tumtum shouted, covered with confusion.

The caretaker fumbled a hand inside the cupboard, trying to find the light switch. He could hear lots of rattling and squealing as General Marchmouse roared commands and shook the bars in the most dreadful rage.

'CHARGE! *CHARGE!*' the General cried. But Tumtum was still holding the ballerinas back. 'How dare you disobey my orders!' the General shouted.

At that moment, there was a sudden clack of high heels, and Miss Short appeared. As she walked past the tuck cupboard, the caretaker looked over his shoulder shiftily. But she took no notice of him.

'Arthur! Lucy! What are you doing here?' she asked crossly. 'Break ended five minutes ago!'

The children at once hurried off to their

classrooms, and then Miss Short disappeared into the staff room.

Finally, the coast was clear.

'*Chaaaarge!*' the General shouted again. And this time they did.

Chapter Fourteen

The caretaker was still fumbling for the light switch when the ballerinas sprang from beneath the locker and began bouncing towards him. They moved in perfect unison, and made not the slightest sound. It was like a silent ballet, with Miss Tiptoe conducting unseen from the rear.

The General was issuing commands through the bars. 'GO! Ambush him now!'

'Stop squeaking!' the caretaker muttered, finally finding the switch. As he turned on the light, the ballerinas all bounced straight for him on their pogo sticks, soaring like a flock of birds towards the huge key ring in his left hand.

The Nutmouses and Miss Tiptoe shook with fear. But the dancers were much too agile for the caretaker. As they rose into the air, they raised their left paws from their pogo sticks and grabbed at the keys as they sailed by, jerking them from his hand. The whole bunch crashed to the floor, with the ballerinas dropping down silently behind.

Before the caretaker had time to look down, the ballerinas had dragged the key ring under the shelf at the back of the cupboard. The Nutmouses were waiting.

'This one!' Tumtum cried, finding a small red key.

'Didn't the gerbils say it was a green key, dear?' Nutmeg asked anxiously.

'No, no – they said it was red,' Tumtum replied. He wrestled furiously to unhook it, sweat pouring down his nose.

'Oh, hurry, Tumtum! Hurry!' Nutmeg squealed. She could see the caretaker looking round in bewilderment. He still had no idea what had hit him.

Finally, the red key fell free.

'Quick! Divert him!' Tumtum shouted to the ballerinas.

Each one of them had a long lace looped round her waist, borrowed from the shoes left in the lockers opposite. Tying one end to the key ring, and attaching the other to their pogo sticks, they all bounced out of the cupboard and made off down the corridor, with the keys clanking and clattering behind them.

The caretaker looked on in astonishment as the ballerinas bounced higher and higher, and faster and faster. He thought he must be seeing things. And yet there they were, as clear as day, *thirteen bouncing mice dressed in beige tutus*!

By the time he had gathered his wits and chased after them, they had bounced nearly as far as the gymnasium.

Meanwhile, the gerbils lowered the ladder, and Tumtum and Nutmeg scrambled up with the red key. 'Hurry up there!' the General said. 'What

the devil's taken you so long? Come on. *Come on!*'

The key was nearly as long as he was, and as Tumtum pushed it into the padlock his paws were shaking. He was normally such a calm mouse, but all the excitement had unnerved him.

Nutmeg placed her paws on his to steady him, and together they tried to turn it in the lock. But though they wriggled it and jiggled it, it wouldn't budge. 'Oh, do move along!' the General bullied, rattling the bars in frustration.

The gerbils were crowded behind him, desperate to get out. But there was nothing the Nutmouses could do. 'We've got the wrong key!' Nutmeg said in despair.

The General turned green. He could hear the other keys clattering further and further away down the corridor, and with them his only hope of freedom. 'Get them back!' he shouted.

Tumtum skedaddled down the ladder and ran recklessly after the ballerinas. 'Come back!' he cried – and hearing him they all obediently turned and raced back down the corridor, pulling the keys behind them.

The girls were at Tumtum's side in seconds. He quickly found the green key and tried to unhook it. But it was wedged tight, and he couldn't prise it off the ring. He could hear the caretaker thundering back up the corridor. He was almost upon them.

'Quick! Tie the whole bunch to the ladder, and we'll pull them up!' shouted the General, monitoring events from the cage.

Trembling, Tumtum tied the keys to the end of the straw ladder with one of the shoelaces. Then the prisoners hoisted them up to the shelf, and Miss Tiptoe and Nutmeg dragged them to the cage.

They found the green key and heaved it up into the lock. Then they wrenched it clockwise, and finally the padlock gave way.

But at that moment a shadow fell over the cage, and, to their horror, the animals saw the caretaker peering in at them. He shot out a hand to snap the padlock shut – but the prisoners moved too fast for him.

'*Charge!*' the General cried; and before the caretaker could secure the lock they all stampeded the door together – a dozen gerbils and their commanding officer bursting free with a great, victorious squeal.

They leapt straight on to the caretaker, and started scrabbling along the arms of his jersey, then cascading down his trouser legs. He swatted at them wildly, but they clung on tight. On reaching the floor they spread into the corridor, hurtling all over the place.

'Scatter!' the General shouted. 'Run for your lives!' The plan had been to retreat through the air vent, but in his excitement the General had forgotten where it was.

Chaos ensued, as ballerinas and gerbils flew about the floor, with the caretaker trying to stamp on them with his enormous boots. The gerbils moved like tornados, amazed at how fast their legs could carry them after their long months in captivity. But the General was so full of humbugs that he was less nimble. 'Give me a pogo stick!' he panted, but there were none to spare.

Tumtum and Nutmeg and Miss Tiptoe crouched under a locker, looking on in dismay. They had promised the General they would follow his orders, but they couldn't understand what he was up to. The operation had descended into chaos.

'Why doesn't he beat a retreat through the air vent?' Tumtum asked hopelessly. 'If this goes on much longer, someone's going to get trodden on.'

Miss Tiptoe decided to take charge. 'He is not fit to lead,' she said sharply, marching out into the corridor.

'Girls! Gerbils! This way, please,' she cried, pointing under the locker with her walking stick. 'Follow me through the vent.'

The girls at once obeyed, and bounced straight towards her. But the gerbils dithered, their loyalties torn. For while they thought the General rather ridiculous, he was an officer, after all, and he was still telling them to scatter.

But then they saw the caretaker's boot looming over them – and without dithering a moment longer they all bolted for cover.

At that moment, Miss Short reappeared.

'They've multiplied!' she shrieked, seeing the animals fleeing under the locker. And then all the classroom doors opened at once, as teachers and children poured into the corridor wondering what the commotion was about.

'You've let them out!' Miss Short raged at the caretaker. 'The whole school will be infested!'

And yet even as she spoke the animals were all escaping through the vent – or at least all but General Marchmouse, for he was so busy shouting commands that he didn't notice the others leaving.

'It's my mouse!' Arthur cried delightedly, seeing the General rushing back and forth in his underpants.

Miss Short let out another shriek, as he darted over her shoe.

'Scatter!' the General cried again, wondering where the others had gone.

'Here, General! Follow us!' shouted Tumtum,

as he hoisted Nutmeg up through the vent.

'How dare you leave the battlefield without my permission!' the General retorted. But then he looked up and noticed for the first time the huge pairs of feet – dozens of them crowded all around him. And suddenly he didn't feel quite so brave.

'Wait for me!' he whimpered, and ran full pelt after the others.

The children all cheered, delighted that their gerbils had escaped being sent to the pet shop.

But Miss Short was furious.

'You may think it's funny now, but just you wait until they multiply!' she snarled. 'They've doubled overnight – I saw at least two dozen of them, and by tomorrow there'll be four dozen,

and by Monday there'll be sixteen dozen, and in a few weeks time there'll be thousands and thousands and thousands of them! And they'll be *everywhere*! You'll find gerbils writhing in your shoes, and burrowing in your pencil cases, and nesting in your coat pockets! They'll take over your desks, and your satchels! And when they die, you'll find their corpses rotting in your food!'

The children looked alarmed, for much as they liked their gerbils, the thought of thousands and thousands and thousands of them was rather unsettling. And the school food was disgusting enough already, without dead gerbils flavouring it.

For a moment, they were all silenced. But

then Lucy noticed something going on outside – it looked as if there were lots of rubber balls bouncing across the playground. She turned and pressed her face to the window pane.

'It's the gerbils,' she said in astonishment. 'They're bouncing!' In fact, it was the ballerinas who were bouncing – the gerbils were running by their side. But they were already too far away for Lucy to tell the difference.

The children crowded round the window to look.

'They're on pogo sticks!' one of them said.

'Don't be ridiculous,' Miss Short snapped. 'Gerbils do *not* use pogo sticks.' But the children sensed that this was not her area of expertise. And from that day on the story of the fantastic bouncing gerbils was to become quite a legend in the village school.

Chapter Fifteen

The animals ran and bounced across the playground as fast as they could, fearing that the caretaker and Miss Short might come chasing after them. It was only when they were outside the school gates that they dared to look round – but the playground was empty, and there was no one coming.

'We've made it!' Tumtum cried. And then all

the gerbils started clapping and whooping – for it isn't everyday that a gerbil escapes.

The ballerinas whooped too – but it was the General who seemed the most excited of all.

'We're free!' he shouted, punching the air in triumph. 'The enemy has been fooled! Oh, what a brilliant campaign! When the Royal Mouse Army hears about this, I shall receive another medal!'

'I say three cheers for Miss Tiptoe and her dancers,' Tumtum said chivalrously. But the General appeared not to hear.

Seeing as the mood was so festive, Nutmeg decided to invite everyone back to Nutmouse Hall. 'We shall have a celebratory feast,' she announced eagerly. And they all thought this was a very good idea – especially the gerbils, for now that they had left the cage, they had no home to go to.

So Tumtum led the party back towards Rose Cottage. It was a slow journey, for everyone was rushing around in different directions, and Miss Tiptoe kept stopping to make sure that none of her dancers had been left behind.

By the time they crawled in under the garden door, it was nearly tea time.

There was no one about, so Tumtum led the party straight across the kitchen floor and under the dresser. Then he held open the gates while they all trooped into the broom cupboard.

When they set eyes on Nutmouse Hall the gerbils suddenly fell quiet. It was like a fairy-tale house, grander than anything they had ever seen, and the sight of so many turrets and windows

overwhelmed them.

When Tumtum showed them inside they were even more astonished. For the gerbils had lived all their lives in one room – and the cage hadn't been much of a room at that. But the Nutmouses had dozens of rooms, all stuffed with treasures. Wherever one looked, there were chandeliers, and tapestries, and pretty vases, and silver candlesticks, and gilt mirrors. There was even a grand piano.

It was all so splendid that the gerbils, who were still naked, felt a little out of place.

But Nutmeg had an idea as to how to make them more at home. 'I'm afraid the house is rather chilly,' she said tactfully, blowing on her paws. 'I think I should find you all something to wear.'

'*Something to wear?*' they asked nervously. The gerbils had never worn anything except the fur coats they had been born in. The idea of clothes struck them as very strange.

But Nutmeg gave them no chance to protest, and promptly shooed them all upstairs for a fitting.

She showed the lady gerbils into her bedroom, and supplied them with pretty frocks and smart cashmere shawls. Then she took the male gerbils into Tumtum's dressing room, and found them each a fine tweed suit.

Once they were dressed in the Nutmouses' expensive country clothes, the gerbils began to feel more sure of themselves.

'Hooray! You look much more civilised,' the General said approvingly as they strutted back into the drawing room. He barely recognised them from the scruffy little creatures he had shared a cage with.

And the gerbils barely recognised the General, for he had not only got dressed, but had brushed his tail and blacked his eyebrows and oiled his whiskers. When he was staying in a smart house he always liked to look his best.

The gerbils and the General had a delightful time admiring each other in the drawing room. And meanwhile Nutmeg set about rustling up a celebratory feast from the odds and ends in her larder.

She made a salmon mousse, and a saffron risotto, and a fish pie, and a bubble and squeak, and a cockroach roulade, and a trifle, and a chocolate mousse, and a sponge pudding with a jug of hot treacle sauce to pour on top.

By the time she'd finished it was getting dark, so she served the meal by candlelight in the banqueting room. And she laid the table with all her best silver and crockery and damask table napkins.

This was a little confusing for the gerbils, who until now had always eaten from a trough. But the ballerinas showed them what to do, and explained how knives were for cutting with, and forks for spearing with, and spoons for spooning with – and the gerbils picked it up so quickly that before long one could hardly tell them from the mice.

Many courses later, as Nutmeg was serving

coffee and mints, Tumtum tapped his glass with a fork, signalling for quiet. Then he stood up heavily, and made an announcement.

'Until you find somewhere to live, you must all stay here with us,' he said addressing himself to the gerbils, who were seated in a long line down one side of the table. 'We've plenty to eat and drink, and we've sixteen spare bedrooms, and nine spare bathrooms, and a ballroom, and a library, and a school room!'

The gerbils raised their glasses and cheered. They were getting so used to all this fine living that their days in captivity already seemed a distant memory.

By now everyone was in such high spirits that no one wanted the party to stop. So after dinner the gerbils and the ballerinas danced together in the ballroom, and it was long after midnight when Miss Tiptoe finally took her charges back to school.

Once the General and the gerbils had gone to bed, Tumtum and Nutmeg made themselves a thermos of cocoa and went to sit in the library. They were unused to entertaining on this scale, and they were both worn out.

'Do you suppose the gerbils will ever move out?' Nutmeg asked, collapsing on to the sofa. She had become very fond of them, but there was a part of her that longed for some peace and quiet again.

'I'm sure we can help them find a proper home of their own,' Tumtum replied reassuringly. 'Rose Cottage is much too small and crowded –

there's not an inch of space left to build in. But there are plenty of nooks and crannies at the Manor House which they could move into. I remember the General telling me about an airing cupboard which the present owners never use. He and Mrs Marchmouse had been going to make their home in it, but they decided it was too big so they took over the gun cupboard instead. It might be just right for the gerbils.'

'Oh, Tumtum, what a wonderful idea!' Nutmeg said happily. 'I'll go up to the attic tonight, and write the children a letter telling them that all the escaped pets are moving into a new home just down the lane.'

Once this problem was solved, the Nutmouses sat silently for a while, watching the fire flicker. They both felt very relieved that all the dramas had come to an end.

'We're such humdrum mice, Tumtum,' Nutmeg said eventually. 'It does seem unfair that we should have been dragged into another adventure quite so soon. I hope we don't have any more.'

'Of course we won't, dear,' Tumtum replied confidently. 'Life will be a lot quieter once the General's safely back in his gun cupboard.'

And Nutmeg hoped very much that Tumtum was right.

The End

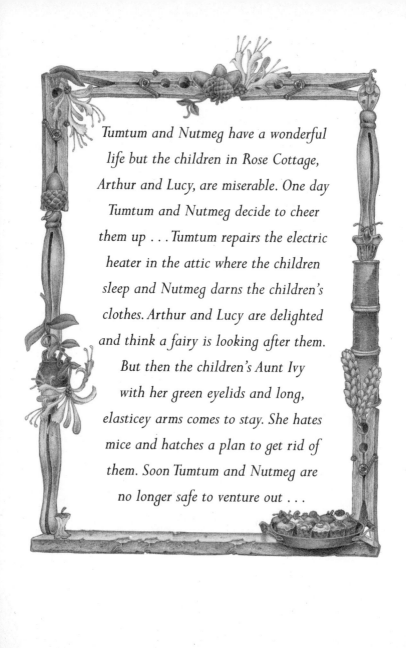

Tumtum and Nutmeg have a wonderful
life but the children in Rose Cottage,
Arthur and Lucy, are miserable. One day
Tumtum and Nutmeg decide to cheer
them up . . . Tumtum repairs the electric
heater in the attic where the children
sleep and Nutmeg darns the children's
clothes. Arthur and Lucy are delighted
and think a fairy is looking after them.
But then the children's Aunt Ivy
with her green eyelids and long,
elasticey arms comes to stay. She hates
mice and hatches a plan to get rid of
them. Soon Tumtum and Nutmeg are
no longer safe to venture out . . .

EGMONT PRESS: ETHICAL PUBLISHING

Egmont Press is about turning writers into successful authors and children into passionate readers – producing books that enrich and entertain. As a responsible children's publisher, we go even further, considering the world in which our consumers are growing up.

Safety First
Naturally, all of our books meet legal safety requirements. But we go further than this; every book with play value is tested to the highest standards – if it fails, it's back to the drawing-board.

Made Fairly
We are working to ensure that the workers involved in our supply chain – the people that make our books – are treated with fairness and respect.

Responsible Forestry
We are committed to ensuring all our papers come from environmentally and socially responsible forest sources.

For more information, please visit our website at
www.egmont.co.uk/ethicalpublishing